PROBATIONARY AGENT

PROBATIONARY AGENT

SCHOOL OF NECESSARY MAGIC RAINE CAMPBELL™
BOOK 08

JUDITH BERENS   MARTHA CARR   MICHAEL ANDERLE

DISRUPTIVE IMAGINATION

LMBPN Publishing
PMB 196, 2540 South Maryland Pkwy
Las Vegas, NV 89109

First US edition, June 2019
Print ISBN: 978-1-64202-343-5

PROBATIONARY AGENT TEAM

Thanks to the JIT Readers

Nicole Emens
Diane L. Smith
Micky Cocker
Dorothy Lloyd
Misty Roa
Shari Regan
Larry Omans
Jeff Eaton
Jeff Goode

If we've missed anyone, please let us know!

Editor
The Skyhunter Editing Team

DEDICATIONS

From Martha

To everyone who still believes in magic
and all the possibilities that holds.
To all the readers who make this
entire ride so much fun.
And to my son, Louie and so many wonderful friends who
remind me all the time of what
really matters and how wonderful
life can be in any given moment.

From Michael

To Family, Friends and
Those Who Love
To Read.
May We All Enjoy Grace
To Live The Life We Are
Called.

CHAPTER ONE

Raine ran her fingers down the spine of the huge tome with a smile and a familiar satisfaction welled up in her. She never experienced the same feeling from her local libraries in Grand Rapids, as wonderful as they were. There was simply an added allure to all the books at the School of Necessary Magic, a special layer to their texture or smell that was almost intoxicating. It wasn't as if they were all ancient or magical, but somehow, sitting in this special library, it was as if they absorbed the atmosphere.

Head Librarian Decker stepped out from between the stacks, a soft smile on his face as he made his way over to her. "You've been back for only a few hours, and you're already in the library? I don't know whether I should be happy or concerned."

"It feels good to be here, and I've not been able to spend as much time in my favorite place during the last couple of semesters." She patted her current book of interest, *Magical Creatures of the Deep Oceans: A Survey of the Western Hemisphere of Oriceran.* "I know all my FBI training is important, but I almost feel like I've neglected this place. I'm sorry, library." She smiled.

The gnome chuckled. "A library exists to serve its readers, and as long as you find value in what there is here, you're not neglecting anything, even if you've been forced by circumstance to spend less time here." The poppy on his hat emitted an odd, rough sound she had never heard before, almost like it was snoring. "And have you never considered becoming a librarian? I'm not criticizing your choice to join the FBI. I'm more interested in satisfying my curiosity and to provide guidance if that's a possible path."

She shook her head. "I like books but being an FBI agent is in my blood. If I tried to not go into the Bureau, I know I'd regret it very quickly, and not only because of my dad. I don't want to call it destiny because that sounds pompous, but it's something like that."

"There are many unpleasant things in this world, Raine, but having solid opinions and options for one's future isn't one of them." He pulled a chair out to take a seat. "And as head librarian, perhaps it is awful of me to say so, but I'm glad you spent this summer having an adventure instead of merely reading about one. Knowledge from academic learning and knowledge from experience enhance each other in a way that makes them both deeper and richer."

"I know." Raine sighed. "I missed having books on hand, though. While I enjoyed helping to add to knowledge with the island survey, I didn't realize how much I missed books until I was away from the island. I suddenly realized I had this huge void only books could fill." She pointed to the cover of her book. "And it's like you say. Academic knowledge helps deepen the experiences. Seeing all those creatures and being on a living island are great memories that I'll never forget, but now, I want to know more. I want to know their history and context in a way the professors didn't explain." She licked her lips. "It's not like they didn't talk about things there, but there wasn't…enough for me. If that makes sense." Her cheeks heated. "I'm not trying to sound ungrateful for what they taught us."

He nodded and his poppy still snored softly. "That makes perfect sense, Raine. It's a question of intensity. You have a keen and thirsty mind. The more I've considered it, the more I think you going into the FBI is perfect for you. Destiny, even." He grinned.

She nodded and didn't bother to hide the surprise on her face. The head librarian had always been supportive throughout her time at the school, but the flow of the conversation had made her think he would seriously suggest she try to consider an alternative path.

"It's hard to be an academic—even a magical academic —without specialization," Head Librarian Decker explained. He held his hand up. A tiny image of a flying red dragon appeared beside a witch carving a complicated glyph into a wall. A swirling portal was the final image.

"That makes sense," she replied, her gaze focused on the images. "There's too much knowledge for a single person to become an expert on in a useful time period. Even if you live a long time, it doesn't mean it won't take you years to learn different things."

"Exactly." He lowered his hand and the dragon disappeared. "So, everyone makes choices about their focus. It's inevitable, but for a very voracious mind, that can feel limiting." A knowing smile followed. "Maybe that's why I ended up a librarian. I never wanted to choose any one path. I have my talents and knowledge, but I'll admit there are many specialists superior to me in both areas." The witch and portal images vanished next.

"But what does that have to do with the FBI?" she asked.

"Cases fall into patterns, but as a magical agent especially, you'll spend decades learning new ways to investigate crimes and different types of magic—an area in which human law enforcement is still woefully behind. You'll have an excuse to constantly expand your mind in different ways without being forced to become as narrow a specialist." Head Librarian Decker gestured around at the stacks holding the books. "The library will be your friend throughout your career, and books will continue to do what they have done during your time here—aid you in making sure justice is done and innocent people are protected."

Raine smiled at her book. "I like the sound of that." Her smile faltered. "And if I get tired of it?"

He released a hearty laugh. His poppy stopped snoring and blew a raspberry.

"Tired of it?" he asked and shook his head. "Maybe you'll tire of the FBI, but you'll never tire of justice, and you're a witch. You'll find there are many ways to extend your life that don't require anything particularly dangerous. I look forward to what you will do in the coming decades, and I know you'll be someone I'll always be proud to have done my small part to help educate."

Her breath caught, and she put a hand over her mouth. She took a few seconds to regain control of her emotions and fight the grateful tears that threatened. "Thank you."

"No, thank you. Remember, at a school, the greatest thing we can run into is students who remind us every day that it's all worthwhile." He touched the rim of his bowler hat and nodded before he stood. "I have a few things to take care of. I'll talk to you later."

She offered him a broad smile and the gnome waved over his shoulder as he wandered away. Several minutes passed as she continued to thumb through her book and soaked in the simple pleasure that came with a quiet room and the pursuit of knowledge. Bright movement and a hint of blue in the corner of her eye caught her attention, and she looked up.

Madelyn entered the library, her flowered pack over her shoulder. She murmured to another gnome near the front before she headed toward a corner reading desk set against a wall. The Coral Elf kept her gaze on the ground the entire time.

Raine drew a deep breath and stood. There hadn't been much time before the end of the semester to get to know Madelyn better, and now that the unusual girl's sister was gone, she needed friends more than ever. Not only that, she had promised Vianna before she died to help her sister.

The elf settled at her desk and removed a small book from her backpack, *The Brothers Karamazov*. Raine raised an eyebrow. She'd not read much classical Russian literature that didn't have to do with magic but was surprised someone so new to Earth would consume something so steeped in a particular history and culture.

She cleared her throat before she was too close to the other girl as she didn't want to startle her. Even if she was less afraid of other students now, she remained skittish. It was easy to look at the teenage-appearing girl and forget she was technically less than two years old. Could magic create true maturity that quickly? She honestly didn't know.

Madelyn's breath caught, and she turned toward Raine. A weak smile appeared. "Oh, hello, Raine."

"Hello, Madelyn," she replied softly. "I was hoping to see you." She forced a bright smile onto her face. "Congrats, you're a sophomore now. That's exciting, right?"

The girl brushed a few stray strands of her blue hair out of her eyes. "Oh, yes, that's true. I hadn't really thought about it. You did that island research project, right?"

Raine nodded. "I'll have to tell you about it. It was kind of crazy with the poachers, and the entire island turned out to be a mallaoch."

Madelyn blinked. "I read about those. I never…" She shook her head. "You seem to get involved in so many crazy things." She gasped and looked at her lap. "I'm sorry. That was rude. I d-didn't think."

"No, it's true." She laughed. "I do get involved in unusual situations because I can't let anything go. In my defense, this time, the trouble came to me. But enough about me. What about you? Did you have a good summer? I thought about you on the trip. We talked about you, too."

Madelyn stared consistently at her lap, her voice even quieter than before. "I…hung out on campus. I read a lot and practiced magic. I've adjusted to being stable, and my magic is now more like true Coral Elf magic." She took a deep breath and raised her head, but she looked at a point beyond her companion's shoulder rather than meet her eyes. "It means some things are harder magically, but some things are easier. I really am a Coral Elf now. Kind of."

"It doesn't matter where you're from. It only matters that you're here now." Raine kept her smile in place. The least she could do for the girl was offer emotional comfort and strength. "You only read and practiced magic?"

"I...talked to Dorvu, too," she whispered. "He's nice. I talked to the library gnomes and some of the professors. They're all pleasant, even if I know some of them don't know what to make of me. I don't think they're afraid of me, but I confuse them."

Raine shrugged. "It's a magic school. We'll always run into new things. Although I can't say I know exactly what it's like to be in your situation, I do know what it's like to enter a whole new world and be unsure of it. But you know what?"

"What?" The elf finally managed to make eye contact. Her differently colored eyes glistened with a hint of tears.

"No matter how uncertain you are, you can get through it. It'll all seem confusing and overwhelming at first, but you'll change from being the girl who doesn't know what's going on to an experienced senior giving people advice, and all that confusion at the beginning will seem weird and hard to relate to."

"Can I really do that without Vianna?" Tears trickled from Madelyn's eyes. "She wasn't only my sister. She was our strength. I'm not strong like you are, Raine. I'm not a real girl. I'm half a soul."

"Don't say that. You are a real girl." She nodded emphatically. "And you can get by the same way everyone without a relative at this school does—with friends. And you have many friends now—not only me but the entire FBI Trouble Squad—and I'm sure you'll make more during your time here." She leaned over to pat the girl's shoulder. "As your friend and a senior, if you need something— anything—come to me. I will help you. I swear it, exactly like I swore to your sister that I would help you."

Madelyn sniffled and wiped her nose as more tears streamed down her cheeks. "T-thank y-you," she stammered.

Raine gave her shoulder a comforting squeeze. "This is the beginning of the rest of your life on Earth, and the professors and the students will do everything we can to make sure it's great."

She continued to sniffle but seemed a little less tense.

Raine risked a quick hug and the elf leaned into it. Sometimes, all a person needed was for someone to show they cared.

CHAPTER TWO

Adrien frowned at the other three boys in his dorm room, his arms folded. Cameron, William, and Philip lounged on the edge of their beds and stared at him with disgusting pity in their eyes. They had looked at him that way since he'd entered the room. He had arrived several hours earlier than the others and had now returned to the room after checking on the Louper equipment, but that was no reason for them to act like they did. He'd missed something, and it gnawed past his restraint and directly to outright annoyance.

"Why?" he demanded. He had reached his limit. "Tell me why."

"Why? What? How?" Cameron shrugged. "Care to finish the question there, Adrien? You sound crazy yelling random questions." He pointed at the wall. "Where?"

Philip snickered.

"Why are you all looking at me like that?" The Light Elf took a deep breath. It wasn't nice to scowl at his friends on their first day back, especially after the glorious summer they had shared. But this was another instance in which he felt like he was a few minutes behind the others when it came to everything that wasn't a fight or Louper. He never held it against his friends, but that didn't make it any less frustrating. Part of being a Guardian involved understanding people, and he acknowledged his slight weaknesses there.

Cameron and William looked at Philip, their eyes pleading.

"What? Seriously?" The wizard rolled his eyes. "You're supposed to be a wolf and an Ifrit, but somehow, you both turned into chickens. Come on."

The shifter shrugged with an apologetic look. William looked away and seemed to suddenly find the wall more interesting than any of his companions.

Adrien's frown deepened. Had he offended them all somehow? He couldn't see how. It wasn't impossible that he might miss something but offending them without knowing it would be rather impressive. They hadn't done much more than exchange pleasantries since his return to the room so there had been no opportunity to do so.

Cameron raised his fist to his face and coughed into it in an obvious stalling tactic. "It's not a big deal. We're worried about you, dude. We want to have your back in this difficult time. You know, Brotherhood of the Room and all that." He nodded, a slight smile on his face. "I wish I had thought of that name earlier."

"This difficult time? Brotherhood of the Room?" The elf lowered his arms and his confusion contorted his face. He ran through everything that had happened on the island and tried to remember if he had said anything that would cause his friends to worry about him, but he couldn't think of anything in particular. They'd departed from one another refreshed and excited about all that had happened. He couldn't have created or chosen a more satisfying summer.

"I don't understand," he said finally. "Why are you worried about me? I'm not joking. I genuinely don't understand."

Philip shrugged. "Because all our girlfriends are still at this school and yours isn't. I never thought much about what it meant that Christie was a year ahead when you got together. I know now that has to suck, especially with how locked-down they have things here, so it's not like you can even grab a phone and call her every night. Painful."

Adrien managed a snicker instead of a loud laugh. He wasn't sure what he had expected, but it wasn't anything about Christie. "That's what you're so concerned about?"

"Well, uh...yeah? Wait. You didn't break up, did you?" The wizard took a deep breath and held it as if awaiting a blow.

"No. Of course not. Why would I break up with such a wonderful girl?" He shook his head, a dismissive smirk on his face as he took a seat. He appreciated his friends' concern, even if it was misplaced.

Philip released the breath he'd held.

"See?" Adrien continued. "You don't have to be concerned."

"Just because you didn't break up with her doesn't mean there's nothing for us to worry about." Cameron frowned. "Of course we'll be concerned. You're our friend. I know you value your privacy, but that doesn't mean we'll simply ignore how hard this might be for you. I know you were okay during the summer, but maybe it really hadn't had time to sink in yet like it will here. It would be hard for me if Raine wasn't here. I'm man and wolf enough to admit that."

William nodded his agreement, a slight frown resting on his face.

"I understand your concern." The elf nodded. "And I appreciate it, but it's misplaced. I won't pretend I won't miss Christie, and I can see myself leaving campus more often than I did last year to contact her, but her absence also solves a problem that would otherwise have been an issue."

"What problem is what?" the half-Ifrit asked.

Adrien pointed to a framed picture on his desk of him with the Louper team at the end of the last season. "We were very close to winning the championship last year. I don't care so much about the undefeated season being lost. This is my last year at this school, and I intend to take the team to the championships and win. That'll require considerable extra dedication from myself and the team, and it means I'll have less free time. It's already been hard to split my time between you, Christie, and the team. Now, I won't have to worry about it as much. I'll graduate with no regrets. I have a duty to her as my girlfriend, but I also have a duty as team captain." He shrugged. "Yes, I'll have Guardian training and work after graduation, but I'll have more than enough time to visit her." A quiet chuckled followed. "Although I wonder if she'll have as much time to visit me."

Philip frowned and leaned forward. "What do you

mean? What's going on with Christie? Isn't she going to college? That's what I heard she would do."

He shook his head. "She changed her mind and decided that four more years of education didn't interest her much."

"Huh," Cameron said and surprise lingered on his face. "What's she up to then?"

"She's an apprentice of sorts." The Light Elf smiled and warmth filled him at the thought of his girlfriend maximizing her career happiness. "Have you ever heard of Looking Glass World Tours?"

The other three boys exchanged looks before shaking their heads.

"Don't feel bad," he said. "I hadn't heard of them either. It's a newer company—only a few years old. They specialize in guided tours. In particular, they specialize in guided cross-world tours. Portal travel is becoming less and less limited, so anyone with a decent amount of resources on either side of the gates can travel to the other world if they wish, but that's not the same thing as knowing where to go and what to see. Many magicals on Oriceran have never been to Earth, and of course, there are billions of people who have never been to Oriceran. There are challenges beyond only the logistical concerns with such tours that require both people skills and magical ability. The company has had difficulty finding recruits on either side for various reasons, so they pay very well and provide comprehensive free training for new employees."

Cameron chuckled. "In the end, she wants to keep leading freshmen around new environments."

"It suits her." William nodded. "She can train while she works and start her own company in the future."

Philip snapped his fingers. "Man, I wish I had thought of a company like that."

Adrien nodded to one of the few other pictures on his desk, Christie smiling in her dress from last year's Spring Formal. "I want her to be happy and live the life that will best make use of her talents, and I think this company is a good way to do that. I will miss her, and I'm sure she misses me, but we're both doing what we need to do at this time, and we'll make sure our time together is that much more special."

The half-Ifrit frowned and looked down. "We'll all have to deal with this next year. Our girls will all go their different ways."

"Yeah, but I agree with Adrien." Cameron grunted and looked away. "I'll admit it's been on my mind a lot with Raine, but I've known she's wanted to go into the FBI from the beginning. I still need to make a few decisions of my own around that, but I'm happy for her."

Philip shrugged. "The way I see it, once we leave this school, a long-distance relationship will be a lot easier. We'll be able to use the train more, and we won't be in a heavily-warded place that messes with communication. Sure, it'll be an adjustment, but it's not possible to actually grow up without having to deal with this stuff."

William blew out a breath and a thoughtful look settled over his face. "That's it, isn't it? We're beginning our senior year, and when the spring semester is over, high school's over." He laughed. "It seems so long ago. Like those Ifrit in the kemana. I was obsessed with that, and now, it's only another thing in my past."

"I came here thinking everyone would hate me as a shifter." Cameron chuckled.

"I was still obsessed with making money." Philip shook his head. "When I think back to some of the stunts I pulled during my first year here, I'm amazed I can show my face to some people." He grimaced.

"We have all grown." Adrien shrugged. "I thought the only thing that really mattered when I came here was learning magic to grow stronger as a Guardian. Even my participation in Louper was fueled somewhat by that, but you and the girls have made me a better elf in all ways."

The boys fell silent while they reflected on how far they had come in their time at the school.

The elf stood and grinned. "We still have an entire year to continue to improve ourselves and plan for the future. I want to be even more worthy of Christie by year's end."

"You're right, dude." Philip nodded. "We need to make this our best year yet for ourselves and our girls."

"We most certainly do."

CHAPTER THREE

Xander murmured a spell as he raised his wand and moved it slowly across the roasted chicken on the modest wooden table before him. He turned his attention to his cup next. Both revealed no reaction—no glowing and no bubbling. It was safe from obvious magical contamination, at least.

The waitress paused at the door to the kitchen, a slight frown on her face before she disappeared inside. A few other customers at the restaurant glanced his way and a Light Elf at a far table scowled deeply. Many magicals considered it rude to leave a wand on a table during a meal, let alone cast a spell over a prepared meal. It implied certain things about the quality.

In all honesty, he didn't care about their dirty looks. The cook at the modest Ruby Falls inn understood his concern wasn't directed against his efforts, which was one of the reasons he frequented the establishment. He couldn't allow himself to be magically poisoned again, especially since the last time, Mara had been the one to have to make a sacrifice to save him. The waitress merely happened to be new. She would learn.

He had dealt with the issue by cutting down on the amount of food and drink he consumed outside the School of Necessary Magic, but that wasn't sustainable. It had been years now, and each passing day fueled more concerns. Although a basic level of paranoia came with being a wizard with his background, at some point, he needed to better determine what had happened and if it would happen again.

His investigations had dead-ended a long time ago. A dark wizard was the obvious candidate, but what he couldn't understand at all was why they had relied on such an indirect method and given up after the single attempt.

The professor set his wand down and picked up his knife and fork to cut into his chicken. He froze and stared as someone he hadn't seen in decades stepped into the restaurant. The new arrival walked with an easy step as if he was a frequent visitor. An overwhelming urge to burst into laughter welled up in Xander but manifested only as a tight smirk. He set his silverware down to lay his hand on his wand. Perhaps his problems were about to solve themselves.

The new arrival—a dark-haired man named Syras—strode in looking very dapper in his suit. It was a far different look than Xander remembered. Before, the man had taken the wizard part of dark wizard seriously. He'd seemed obsessed with the idea that looking like a stereotypical robed wizard was the first step to the dark wizards separating themselves from their alleged inferiors and controlling the world.

Syras' gaze swept the room. It settled on the man who stared at him and recognition and something else—disappointment, perhaps— manifested in his eyes.

His fingers tightened on his wand, but he kept it on the table and simply waited as the newcomer strode toward him. The other wizard's arms remained at his side as he walked. His wand had to be inside his jacket, but it would only take seconds to pull it out and cast a spell. All Xander's anti-poison efforts wouldn't save him from a fireball in the chest.

The dark wizard stopped at the table and nodded to an empty chair. "It's been a long time."

"Yes, it has." The professor refused to blink. "You were the last person I expected to see here tonight. I happened to think about something similar, so maybe I nudged the universe along. It would be nice to think I've earned a little of that."

"I'm not here to cause you trouble." Syras sat slowly, his hands in front of him and his attention now focused on the other man's wand. He folded his hands and set them on the table. "I'm really not. I do think you should cast a silence spell before we continue, though. What I have to say isn't for others, but it's your choice. You made that clear when you walked away from us."

He uttered a quiet chuckle. "You'll let me cast a spell when you're not shielded and you don't have a wand out?" He didn't sense much magic from the wizard. If he depended on an artifact, there should have been a stronger signature. "You're far braver than I remember."

"Many things have changed over the years." Syras shook his head. "And we both know you're not a man given to casual violence. Cast the spell, and we'll talk."

Xander raised his wand. He allowed himself a blink but refused to take his gaze off his unexpected visitor. Someone had poisoned him three years before, and the dark wizard he knew from the old days who suddenly appeared when least expected was the best candidate thus far. After a quick flourish and an incantation, the slight background murmur of the inn died away.

"I could have killed you right there." He narrowed his eyes. "You might have improved in technique over the years, but so have I, and I was stronger and better, to begin with."

"You have no reason to kill me." The wizard sighed. "I was never your enemy. I understood why you turned your back on us, and I made that clear to the others."

"Maybe you changed your mind." He didn't lower his wand.

"If I wanted to kill you, would I approach you in public without my wand ready? Does it make sense? Would it be good tactics?"

Xander took several deep breaths before he slid his wand back into a holster inside his jacket. "Probably not. You always were painfully straightforward, Syras. I always appreciated that about you, but you also have to realize that it's a little suspicious when you show up here, of all places, when we haven't talked in a long time."

Syras shook his head at the approaching waitress. She rolled her eyes and moved on to another table.

"I'm not here by chance," he said. "So it's good to be suspicious." He gestured toward the wand. "You weren't the kind of wizard before who would eat with your wand at the ready, so that makes this easy because it means you still take the poisoning seriously."

Xander's jaw tightened. "You know about that?"

"I've heard things, yes."

"And you had nothing to do with it?"

The wizard snorted. "Poison's a coward's weapon." He closed his eyes and sucked in a long, deep breath. "And, no, I had nothing to do with it. If anything, I'm here because I want to avoid you being killed. I've never forgotten what you did for me in Lima. Those Griffins would have killed me if it weren't for you. Maybe you don't think it was a big deal, but I do. And I know Hadrian wanted you to leave me behind."

"Hadrian was always self-serving." He nodded slowly. "And we were friends at the time. I haven't regretted it—yet. Don't make me think Hadrian was right."

"I'm not here to make you regret it. I'm not like some of the others from back in the day. It's unfortunate you gave up on our cause. I believe, deep down, that you'll realize your mistake and come back to the right side of history, but to do that, you need to still be alive."

"Okay, I'm listening." He finally shifted his gaze from the man to check around the room for anyone else who looked suspicious. A few annoyed patrons glared at him, displeased with his dining room faux pas, but no one looked like they were about to join an ambush.

Syras leaned forward and an even more serious expression filled his face. "When I heard about the poisoning, I assumed it was a one-off—someone you pissed off back in the day or who didn't like you leaving the cause behind. But I've heard a few things recently that make me think something else is going on. I also heard a few rumors about someone asking around about you. I tried to find out who, but they went through considerable effort to remain anonymous—disguise spells, anti-tracking, and the rest. I don't know who they are."

Xander reached for his wand again. "I want to use a truth spell."

"Fair enough. I would if I were you."

He made a few quick movements and chanted the spell. A small orb appeared. "Okay, talk."

"Marlan, Devon, and Aria," Syras declared.

The orb remained unchanged. The names were familiar as Xander had been close to them in his days of dark magic, but like any recovering addict, he had been forced to leave the friends associated with his addiction behind when he walked away from the dark magic. Hadrian and Syras were also close friends from that period, among others, but he'd already drifted away from both of them even before he cut his old ties for different reasons.

"What about Marlan, Devon, and Aria?" he muttered. "I'm sure they have many interesting complaints about me, but I made it clear to them when I stepped away from all of it. They stay out of my way, and I'll stay out of their way. I have a good thing at this school, and I won't let anyone destroy it regardless of what they think they're doing for the future—even if that means going up against old friends."

"They won't mess with you, Xander."

He smirked. "Oh. They're that afraid of me?"

"No." Syras sighed and looked down. "They're all dead."

"What?" He didn't bother to try to keep the surprise from his face.

The wizard looked up. "Can I be any clearer? They're dead."

"I didn't know. I don't...keep in contact with people from the old days."

"I know." The man frowned. "Someone's hunting dark wizards. Someone with a grudge."

Xander released a bitter chuckle. "There are many people with those."

"Here's the strange thing. When I started investigating, I noticed a pattern, and that makes me worried." Syras leaned back, his brow creased in a frown. "Because you won't see it coming."

"They were all poisoned?" He scoffed.

Syras shook his head. "As far as I heard, you were the only one. I know some of the others wanted to reach out to you after that, but they didn't because they didn't think you would want to talk to them."

"They were right. I don't understand the pattern other than we knew each other before and did things together." He stared at a flickering orb that floated on the edge of the room, a spell meant for mood more than real illumination. "It's not like I can possibly go after everyone we might have annoyed back then. I wouldn't even know where to start or remember everyone."

"That's not the issue. Marlan died from a slow-acting magical disease four years ago. You were poisoned three years ago. Devon was cursed with a wasting spell two years ago. Aria died from some sort of rapid-aging spell that turned her days into years." Syras frowned. "It seems like everyone died a slow death—everyone but you, and you were on your way at first."

"And do you think you're next?" Xander raised a questioning eyebrow.

Syras took a deep breath and locked eyes with him. "I was never as close as the rest of you. I always knew that. So did everyone else. I don't think they'll attack me next." He gestured toward the truth orb. "I think they'll attempt to kill you again. I don't know why whoever did this didn't simply do so at once. Maybe they want you to be afraid."

The truth orb hadn't changed at all during the conversation. He didn't dismiss it, even though the number of disgruntled looks had only increased since he cast the spell.

Xander snorted. "I didn't even know about the others."

"The killer might not have known that. They've gone through the others, and that means they could target you again. They'll try to finish what they started before." Syras licked his lips. "I'm sorry, Xander, but whoever did this has managed to assassinate three powerful dark wizards and almost killed a fourth. I can't be the fifth." He stood. "I've done my part. I've paid you back for Lima, but until you stop this person, I can't be seen around you anymore."

"And if they kill me, too?"

"I'll send flowers to your funeral." The wizard nodded. "You can run from the past, but it has a nasty habit of catching up with you." Without looking back, he strode toward the exit.

Xander canceled his truth and silence spells. Syras was right. He had only survived because the most important person in his life had cared enough about him to make her own sacrifice. This time, he would not allow her to make another.

CHAPTER FOUR

Mara leaned back in her chair as she stared at Xander from behind her desk. He had finished explaining the situation to both her and Bruce and in a strange way, she was almost relieved. The almost effective attempt on his life and the lack of follow-up left a splinter of lingering concern in her mind. They might have some chance to finally resolve the problem if the enemy was on the move again.

"I don't know what this all means," the wizard said with a shrug. "Syras could be wrong. It might very well be that no one has targeted me. They might have made their single attempt three years ago and have given up. Logically, they could have tried again instead of moving on to the others if they wanted to."

Bruce cleared his throat. "I doubt that. Even if it involves magical curses, if your associate is right about everything that has happened with the others, you either have someone very patient or a serial killer, but the specificity of the targeting suggests this is more personal."

Xander chuckled. "I'm glad you said that, because I feel the same way, but I wanted to present the other option."

She frowned. "And you're sure it's not Syras?"

He nodded. "I used a truth spell. While I didn't check for an artifact, I didn't sense much magic off him. It's not impossible that he obscured the truth, but I did save his life in Lima years ago. Vengeance against someone who saved your life doesn't make much sense."

"Let's assume it's not him," the other man said, his face stony. He now operated in FBI agent mode. She wasn't sure if that comforted her or worried her more. "We'll assume for the moment he's exactly what he appears to be —a helpful informant."

"If it's not Syras, who could it be?" Mara asked.

Bruce nodded. "A suspect list would be helpful. We could begin to narrow down their movements and current locations, and we can better anticipate any potential attacks that way."

Xander laughed. "What good is a list that's filled with dozens of people from decades ago? Maybe even more. I had a considerable number of enemies in my past, and then I made more when I tried to break with that." He gestured around the room. "At least we know that no professor on this campus wants to kill me. Maybe Leo does, depending on the day of the week. I did keep that one book out way past its due date, but poison's rather extreme to punish me for a late book."

"This is serious, Xander," she snapped. "Someone tried to kill you, and they may make another attempt."

"I know it's serious." He drew a deep breath. "And the reason I've told you this is that even though I want help, I also don't want any above and beyond heroics this time." He gave her a meaningful glance. "I also don't intend to sit around and get picked off. Whoever is doing this is patient, and if I'm the next target, I'd rather make myself the bait and let their arrogance lead them to expose themselves. Then, I can stop them and determine what this is about, or at least end any future attempts on my life."

The agent shook his head. "You can't guarantee they'll use the same tactics. For all you know, next time, they'll use a bomb spell. They might be frustrated about their earlier failures and willing to change."

"Frustrated but simply move on to someone else? That doesn't make a lot of sense, and after everything Syras told me, I doubt whoever wants to kill me would be satisfied with me dying quickly from a bomb. It sounds like they want me to suffer." Xander's grin was perversely merry. "That gives me an opportunity to pay back my secret admirer for what they put me through the first time."

"The other thing I'm confused about is why now?" Bruce asked. "It's been years since you left your old life behind. Whether it's another dark wizard or someone who felt victimized by you, why wait all this time?"

Mara and Xander both pondered that in silence, but it was the headmistress who answered. "Being able to accomplish the dangerous and powerful magic required to kill three others and almost kill Xander isn't trivial. One possibility is that it might have taken them decades of study or research to develop the necessary magical skill." She looked at Bruce. "It's not always simply about finding the right artifact."

Discomfort played across his face, but he managed to

mask it. "That's considerable effort, then, and it also goes to motive." He looked at the wizard. "And you don't know of anything your little group did to anyone in particular that would elicit that kind of revenge?"

"Honestly, I don't know." The wizard stared off into the distance, a haunted look in his eyes. "I'll never deny that I became overwhelmed by dark magic and did things I'm not proud of, but nothing that would drive someone to hunt me and the others for decades. Not this long. And it's not as if the other targets and I were some dark magic FBI Trouble Squad always hanging out together. We did associate a fair amount for a few years, but we often drifted in and out of contact, even before I left dark magic behind."

"Then if not a victim, maybe it's a political rival." Bruce shrugged. "Dark wizards don't always get along."

"Sure, but assassinating multiple wizards with this kind of magic?" Xander shook his head. "It goes against everything the dark wizards stand for. Yes, they can let dark magic overwhelm them, but you always have to remember, the point is supposed to bring about order and pride in the old families. It'd be one thing if a wizard ended up dead in the back room of a kemana inn under mysterious circumstances, but these murders scream for reprisal. It's the kind of thing that creates fractured alliances and internal strife. There's so little to gain from it and so much to lose, as it only risks disrupting carefully laid plans."

The agent shook his head. "I've seen people risk more for less during my years in the FBI. Magic doesn't change the fundamental nature of a person. It simply gives them more tools to cause trouble. In the end, it comes down to the same kinds of passions—greed, anger, envy, and the like."

"I don't know what to tell you. I have no idea who it might be. All I know is there's a good chance they'll make another attempt, and I refuse to let them win." Xander narrowed his eyes and curled his hand into a fist. "They had their chance, and they failed. Well, if they try again, so be it. I'm tired of checking my meals for poison when I leave the school grounds. I owe them for the first time, let alone any other time."

Mara took a deep breath. "There's another obvious risk we need to discuss, and we might as well do that now."

Both men looked at her and curiosity replaced the concern on their faces.

She gave the wizard an apologetic look. "I'm sorry, but if someone has targeted you, we have to ask ourselves if it puts the school and the students at risk. After what happened with Eris, let alone a few years ago, I'm concerned. Our students are safe on school grounds, but unless we keep them here, there's always a vulnerability. I'm wondering if this potential attack represents a risk."

Bruce nodded. "Maybe we should consider restricting them to school grounds."

Xander shook his head. "For how long? The entire year? No. It'll compromise their education, and I don't think it's necessary. We might not know who is behind these attacks, but we do know their tactics and their targets. If they didn't care about collateral damage, they wouldn't have relied on the poison. We shouldn't involve the students in this, even indirectly. There's no reason for them to be concerned about something that only affects me."

The headmistress considered that, her hands folded in front of her and discomfort rampant in her mind. Some things were beyond her control, no matter what she was willing to sacrifice. "I agree for now. If we have any indication that this is a more general risk, we'll consider changing our approach."

The wizard shook his head. "Not necessary."

The agent frowned. "The safety of the students has to come first."

"I agree, but if it comes to that, I'll simply leave the school." Xander stared at Mara. "No one else I care about will be made to suffer for my mistakes."

The other man nodded but concern lingered on his face. "Then let's concentrate on catching the killer before they finish the job."

Mara released a breath she didn't even know she was holding. "I agree."

CHAPTER FIVE

Raine waited patiently at a table near the front as Professor Powell paced and tapped his wand on his leg, an odd expression on his face. It was as if he was nervous about something, but she'd never seen him all that concerned in class, even when they learned dangerous spells. She decided she simply saw something that wasn't there, a tendency Agent Connor had warned her against.

"Over the last several years, I've taught you many different ways to protect yourself." He raised his wand. "I've taught you offensive spells and defensive techniques, and we'll definitely continue with that this year. Every spell I teach you is a new tool in your arsenal, and each provides you with a way to survive an encounter. You never know what and who you'll run into out there. The world isn't necessarily a dangerous place overall, but there are many dangerous people in it."

She nodded slowly and thought back to their encounter with the chaos witch. She would never have thought that a slime spell would prove the key to victory. Adrien's mastery of burst spells had helped him not only in Louper but in several FBI Trouble Squad fights. Similar things could be said about the others. Unlike most students in that room, they understood what it meant to have their lives on the line and how important the wizard's lessons were.

None of her close friends were in her defense against dark magic section this semester with the exception of Adrien, who was even more intense and focused than usual. She didn't mind, as being obsessed with a class was something she could share with him.

Juniper sat a few tables away and elicited her sympathy. The other girl had originally been scheduled to go on the summer research trip along with Raine and her friends but had to pull out at the last moment. Malcolm had suffered the same fate. Having to help apprehend poachers might have given them more insight into Professor Powell's classes.

Everyone knew about the huge battle that had taken place before Raine had started at the school, but most acted like it was something decades in the past—a dusty concern for history books, not living history that could have involved them. They believed the wards would save them. Dark wizard spies couldn't achieve that sort of thing again, others said. Confidence filled the students. Even the recent efforts of the chaos witch Eris were passed off as an aberration, a passing danger that would never return.

But Raine knew the truth. Every magical needed to be able to defend themselves because not every other magical was a good person. She couldn't do much about that on anything other than a personal scale until she joined the

FBI, but she would make sure she lasted long enough to accomplish it.

"For this unit," Professor Powell continued, "I want to take advantage of your advanced knowledge of illusion techniques to help you with some quicker spells that can be useful in a fight. Have any of you heard of a multi-fake?"

Her hand shot up on reflex. He grinned and pointed to her.

"It generates copies of the caster," she explained. "But they move around on their own—not much, but enough so it's not totally obvious who the original is. In that sense, it's a defensive spell or a funny spell for a trick."

A few of the other students laughed.

He nodded. "Exactly. It's fairly quick to cast compared to true illusion spells. But it requires precise movements, incantations, and difficult magical energy management, which is why we don't teach it until senior year." He pointed his wand at a gray-haired elf near the back, Jillian. "Speaking of tricks, I'm sure other applications besides battle might come to mind depending on your hobbies."

This time, the entire class laughed. Even though the Live Unnecessary Tricksters were supposed to be a secret society, everyone at the school knew their members and that Kayla was the current leader of the prank squad. While the group had experienced a few dangerous close calls thanks to the chaos witch's efforts to disrupt magic at the school last year, only their honorary member Sara had given up on pranks.

Jillian scoffed and shrugged. "I wouldn't know, Professor."

He smirked. "I'm sure you wouldn't." He turned to the

rest of the class. "Now, I said it's fairly quick to cast, but that's a relative judgment. It's not something you can quick-chant like a fireball spell, which means if you're already in the middle of a fight, it's probably too late to use it. But if you know you're about to step into one, it can be useful." He pointed his wand at his chest. "As I mentioned earlier, careful energy management is required, so it can be difficult to maintain it while stacking other spells. It's something you'll have to evaluate on a situation-by-situation basis."

Adrien frowned from where he sat at the side of the classroom. "It doesn't sound as useful as simply using shield spells."

"Oh?" Professor Powell pointed his wand to his side and made a few quick movements while he chanted what sounded like an image spell to Raine. A tall, broad-shouldered man appeared. His mutton chops and top hat suggested someone from the nineteenth century. "Tell it to Damian Blackwell."

"Who?" The elf's face scrunched in confusion.

Raine recognized the name immediately. There were advantages to being obsessed with reading in a magical library. "He was a Silver Griffin who was mostly active in the nineteenth century. They called him the Indefatigable Hunter."

"The Indefatigable Hunter?"

She shrugged. "It was the nineteenth century. I'm sure it sounded cool back then."

"Yes," the professor said. "He was involved in many dangerous situations with magicals who didn't agree with much of the magical control policies. I know it's sometimes hard for you to appreciate, but just because there were rules and restrictions against open magical use didn't mean people didn't try to break those rules. Then again, you're students, so you might relate to that better than I can."

The class laughed.

Professor Powell smiled. "Damian found himself on the trail of a few rogue wizards who had experimented with dangerous summoning rituals that not only killed people but risked exposure of the magical world. He was alone at the time but found their hideout. Unfortunately, he realized that if he waited, they might get away, so he made his move. He used a multi-fake to deceive them all before he launched his attack. The final result was one Silver Griffin who took down seven rogue wizards because they couldn't identify their true adversary."

Adrien smiled, his face filled with respect for the historical figure. There was a hint of something in the professor's eyes, an amusement that Raine didn't fully understand, but she didn't want to press him on it. Professor Powell, like all the staff, had many secrets he probably didn't want to share with the students.

"Okay," he continued and raised his wand. "Let's get to the spell itself. The initial key is to gather the magical energy. You'll need to break it apart into a few different streams, similar to how I've shown you on previous spells. Those separate energy flows will be needed for the different images." He performed a few precise movements with his wand, the magic invisible but easy for everyone in the room to sense. "Then, it's a matter of the incantation, along with concentrating on the kinds of things you want the images to do. It doesn't have to be exact, of course. The spell will take care of some of that, but if you're too unfocused, you'll have weird effects." More wand work followed as he slowly and loudly enunciated the incantations.

Four new Professor Powells winked into existence. Two of them frowned and folded their arms, while their gazes swept the classroom as if disappointed. Another crept forward, his wand at the ready as if he intended to launch a spell into the back of the room. The last fake mirrored the stance of the original, including when he scratched his eyelid.

"As you get better with the spell," he explained, "you'll be able to create more complicated fakes. Note that it's not as all-encompassing as an illusion and far easier to see through, if only because of the obvious magic from the fakes, but also, this spell doesn't create accompanying sounds either." The fake Powell continued to creep forward and shimmered as he passed through the edge of a table. "But like Damian Blackwell, if you use it in the right situation, it can be very effective." He cut through the air with his wand, and his fakes disappeared. "Now, we'll practice and try it out after I explain how those without wands need to modify their technique."

Two copies of Adrien darted among the desks, each with a sword in hand. The original stood in a corner, crouched and ready. Leave it to the Guardian trainee to practice the technique with all the seriousness he brought to everything else in his life.

Several students clapped. He was one of the first to create decent motion with his copies. A few more seconds of triplet actions continued before the fakes disappeared and he sat with a pleased expression.

"Very good," Professor Powell said and clapped lightly. "Raine, I'd like you to go next."

She half-closed her eyes, her fingers tight around her wand. While she was able to hold onto three decent flows of magical energy, it seemed to take all her concentration. A few deep breaths followed before she raised her wand and initiated her incantations.

Three blonde versions of her appeared. She grimaced and stumbled back. Her copies all matched her movements but not her appearance. Her spell was less multi-fake than strange funhouse.

One of them was a lanky, too-thin form several feet taller than her. Another was stout with an unnaturally wide mouth and uneven eyes. The third was the right size and shape but lacked a mouth.

She sighed and released her images. "That will definitely not help."

The professor shook his head. "You would be surprised how in battle, many people aren't as detail-focused as you might believe. Simply having additional targets helps, especially if they move. If you paid close attention to Adrien's fakes, you would have noticed several key details were off, such as color patterns. One even had a different sword."

The elf's face tightened.

Professor Powell put a hand out and shook his head.

"It's not a criticism. You did very well for your first real time—and for that matter, no one else even noticed, which only goes to reinforce my point." Once the student nodded in response, the professor turned toward Juniper. "It seems like you're ready. Please give it a try."

The dark-haired girl smiled and raised her head and confidence radiated off her face. Her wand movements were dramatic and her incantations loud. Everything built to a stronger performance than Adrien's.

The entire class inhaled a sharp breath when the chickens appeared—six in all, three roosters and three hens. The birds wandered near Juniper's feet and pecked at the floor.

She blinked at her new flock. "Huh? Chickens?"

Snickers among the class turned into full-blown laughter. The silent birds continued their mindless meander and ignored their creator. A few details were off—odd patterns in their feathers and the wrong color of eyes on a few—but from a distance, they resembled a realistic group of chickens. Unfortunately, they weren't exactly the most useful multi-fakes in a fight unless you faced other hostile fowls.

Juniper's cheeks reddened, but her expression remained more confused than embarrassed. "I don't understand why they're chickens." Her stomach rumbled. "Oh, maybe that's why."

Professor Powell grinned. "I'm surprised you didn't end up with rotisserie versions."

CHAPTER SIX

Raine took a bite of her grilled chicken and tried to ignore the faint sense of guilt that rose after what had happened in class. There was no reason why she shouldn't eat the meal, but she hadn't wanted chicken for lunch until Juniper's mistake. She glanced around to make sure the other girl wasn't anywhere near. It had been a mistake any of them could have made and she didn't want her to feel self-conscious.

The food, as usual, was delicious. She thought about what the meal situation would be like at the FBI Academy. There wouldn't be any pixies, and she doubted it would be the same quality. In many ways, despite the dangers she had experienced during her time at the School of Necessary Magic, it was a sheltered existence. She was surrounded by instructors and students who were all magicals, and she lived in an expanded magical mansion. Her return to something more mundane during breaks wasn't the same as the harsh reality of being one of the first magicals to openly attend the FBI Academy.

Raine wasn't afraid, even if they had terrible food. Her whole life had led her to Quantico, and even though she knew it would be tough, it would also be worth it in the end. She wouldn't disappoint her parents, Uncle Jerry, Agent Connor, or any of the others who had believed in her even when she had been unsure of herself. She blinked a few times and tried to refocus on the table conversation.

"I've considered adjusting some of our play strategies going forward." Adrien finished his explanation to Philip. "If we want to take the championship, it'll be necessary. We're too defensive. Everyone's skills are improving, and we have a much deeper bench this season, so I want to sub more. But we also lost some of our most experienced players with graduation, and I need to take that into account."

The wizard nodded eagerly. "I know you can do it, dude. Sure, you might not have Daniel and Cody anymore, but every school lost seniors too. Remember that."

"True enough." The Light Elf frowned. "I'm eager to face off against Orono."

Cameron grinned. "Do you want to see if Finn will take it easy on you?"

He snorted. "I hope not. That would be an insult. I'll destroy him, and I hope he tries to do the same to me."

Raine swallowed another bite of chicken and searched the dining hall for Madelyn. One easy way to help the girl was to share meals with her. It was a low-stress way to socialize and get to know people better, even if all she did was sit there and eat her food.

"Has anyone seen Madelyn?" she asked.

The others all looked around and shook their heads.

"I saw her coming out of the library earlier," Evie said, concern in her eyes. "I said hi, and she said hi back, but she seemed like she was in a hurry. Is everything okay? She seemed fine. Shy, but then she always is."

"It's fine." She sighed. "I don't like her to eat alone, that's all. I've tried to think of ways to interact with her more, but it's hard because she's only a sophomore and we don't have any of the same classes."

Sara smirked from beside Philip. She held her fork up and pointed it menacingly. "Recruit her next time something dangerous happens. We could use another elf on the squad."

Adrien, Cameron, and Philip snickered.

"Nothing dangerous will happen," Raine said. "It's our senior year, and they've strengthened defenses here because of what happened with Eris."

"Really? You think nothing will happen?" The kitsune flashed her an incredulous look. "We haven't gone a single semester at this school without something dangerous happening—or at least something we thought was dangerous. We couldn't even go through last summer without having to apprehend criminals who were more than happy to kill us all. I don't know what it is, but it's like we're cursed to always be involved in trouble." She shrugged. "Or blessed, depending on how you look at it."

William shrugged. "We are the FBI Trouble Squad."

"It's because a certain someone can't ever ignore anyone in trouble." Cameron patted Raine on the shoulder. He lowered his hand and a smile built. "I say that, but it's all of us, really."

Adrien considered the statement before he nodded.

"True enough. We've all had our chances to walk away and not get involved. We've always chosen not to."

"There's nothing wrong with helping people." Evie punctuated her sentence with a sip of juice.

The shifter's expression turned serious. "And let me be clear, I think it's a good thing—for Raine and the rest of us. I've often thought about everything that's happened at this school since we started here, and I feel like we've left it a better place. Now, I do sometimes wish Raine would dial it down, but I'm proud she has helped so many people."

Raine smiled at her boyfriend and warmth suffused her body. "No, I agree. I'm not saying I've never been scared—whether it was the druids or Eris—but I don't ever regret risking myself to help other people." She sighed and her shoulders slumped. "But none of that changes the fact that I don't have good ideas for Madelyn right now. I thought about something like Student Council, but there is too much argument, and you always have at least one rude, bossy type on the council. She doesn't seem to have any hobbies other than reading."

"Of course she doesn't," Philip said. "She's still technically a toddler. Or is she a baby? Babies don't have hobbies."

Sara shook her head. "I don't think you can really judge her by her age like that."

Evie nodded her agreement.

Adrien frowned, his expression thoughtful. "Her motor skills make her not a toddler."

Cameron and William both snickered but didn't add to the discussion.

Raine turned to the side at a flash of blue, only to

realize it was a pixie demonstrating a pulsating orb spell for a new student. "She's not technically a baby, but she still has a lot to learn about the real world and she doesn't have the emotional defenses yet that allow her to take risks. Let's face it, there have always been more than a few bullies at this school."

"If someone's bullying her, they'll have to deal with us." Sara glowered and smacked her fist into her palm. The others nodded their agreement.

"You're right, of course, but that's not what I'm talking about. I need something more concrete to help her grow socially. I know some of the professors are trying, but they can't always relate even to us, and we're closer to them in age and mindset than Madelyn is."

"Louper," Adrien declared, his face a mask of certainty. "It's hard to be in the Louper stands and not be caught up in the excitement. Having the school to cheer for provides a natural support group."

"He's right," Cameron said. "Encourage her to go to Louper matches. Even when I was still getting comfortable with everyone, I felt at home during Louper matches."

"Same here," William said.

Raine smiled. "That's a good idea. They can get fairly loud, but I'll work with her on a sound dampening spell. Given how much she and Vianna used to sneak around, she might already know them. Louper. Okay, that's one idea, but it's not like we have Louper all the time."

"The world can't be so perfect." Philip sighed.

Evie's face scrunched in heavy concentration. "I could invite her to bake with me."

Sara looked away and paled. "She doesn't have witch

magic. Isn't her magic more water and ice based? I know she's not a true Coral Elf, but everything they said made it sound like she might as well be."

"Sure, but she doesn't have to use magic when she cooks."

"It's just…if something goes wrong, strange things can happen." The kitsune shuddered.

Evie gasped and put a hand to her mouth. "Sentient cupcakes from a girl who was made from a game?"

"Maybe."

"No baking."

Sara nodded vigorously. "That's a good idea."

"Maybe she wants to help with charity work." Philip smiled. "She can learn more about people and improve her social skills."

Raine shook her head. "I think it'd be hard since she's still very shy, but maybe it's something I can suggest to her for next year."

The wizard bolted out of his chair. Students at several other nearby tables stared at him, surprise or amusement on their faces.

"I am a genius," he declared before he dropped into his seat again. "I am a total genius. Sometimes, I impress even myself."

Sara rolled her eyes. "Is this really the time for jokes?"

"No, you don't get it." He rubbed his hands together, his face alight with glee. "I had the ultimate idea. It's an easy activity that's low stress for Madelyn, where she gets to socialize with all of us and, at the same time, learn about the two worlds in different contexts." He grinned. "Can't you think of something we do like that?"

"Movie nights!" the entire table shouted at once.

A kitchen pixie flew past and wagged her finger. "Let's keep it under control. Just because you're seniors now doesn't mean you run this school."

"Sorry," Raine said and her cheeks heated. "We all got excited."

"Students are always excited," mumbled the pixie as she flew away.

"She can use the movies to help learn what it means to be human," Philp explained.

Adrien cleared his throat. "Keep in mind that not only did she not come into the world the same way as us but, for that matter, her current form isn't human."

"Oh, right, sorry. I only want to help her. Should we try to find other Coral Elves to come and talk to her?"

Adrien sighed. "I'm sure the staff has considered it, but that's not necessarily a good idea either. She might have a Coral Elf form, but she wasn't raised as one, nor does she share their culture. In a sense, she's probably more comfortable with the races in this school than she would be with a true Coral Elf."

Philip waved his hand. "Whatever. The movie idea is great. Sure, we watch a lot of human- and English-centric movies, but she has to start learning somewhere. If she needs help to choose movies, we can do that, or maybe she has movie tastes already. So, she watches movies, and since we discuss them at the end, she'll always understand how normal..." He frowned and seemed to consider his words carefully. "Uh...how born people normally think about the stuff in the movies." He shrugged. "And we can learn more about how she thinks by the types of movies she chooses and adjust based on that."

"She seems comfortable enough around all of us, and other people don't go in the room." Raine looked at her friends for any sign of discomfort, but everyone seemed excited by the idea, even Adrien—by his standards, at least, which meant he smiled slightly. "I'll find her in the library later and invite her to the next movie night." She made a face. "Just a suggestion for the first night she comes—no horror."

CHAPTER SEVEN

A few days later, the friends wandered the narrow streets of Ruby Falls, taking in the stalls filled with colorful fruits, jewelry, charms and other bric-a-brac for sale. The only person missing was Adrien, who had scheduled an extra Louper practice. His main goal for the year had already consumed his school life.

An entire board of glowing crystals lay beside a blanket covered in hollowed gourds in a variety of colors. It was difficult to say anymore what might look natural or unnatural given some of the oddities of plant life on Oriceran. The kneeling female dwarf vendor smiled invitingly and nodded to her goods.

Raine shook her head politely as the group moved on. All the pretty baubles and strange Oriceran imports in the kemana couldn't exorcise one lingering thought that had clouded her mind. "I can't believe Madelyn said no to movie night. It was such a great idea."

Sara shrugged. "You made the offer. That's all we can

do. If we try to force her, it'll work against what we're trying to do. We want it to be fun, not some new scary event that's only more stress for her. We don't want to come off like bullies."

"I understand that, but I wonder if we should have invited her here." She sighed. "I know she's been here before."

"Maybe she isn't allowed," Cameron said. "The PDA might have special rules."

"I honestly don't know."

A gnome in a cowboy hat and matching attire, complete with leather chaps, crossed the street in front of her. He glanced their way and tipped his hat to the group before he moseyed on. There was always something memorable to see in the kemana.

"I don't know if this place has good memories for her," William said. "Every time she came here before, it was with Vianna, right? It might be a good thing to avoid it, and it can get rowdy. Even if we set aside the fact she's still in mourning, it'll take a while for her to come out of her shell without the other literal half of her soul around."

"That makes sense." Raine sighed. "You know me. I simply see someone who needs help, and I want to throw myself constantly at the problem until I solve it."

"That's not a bad thing, Raine," Sara said. "But keep in mind most of this needs to come from Madelyn. All we can do is hold our hands out. She still has to choose to take them. Change begins within. That's something we've all learned at the school."

Cameron, who had walked a few feet ahead, stopped

abruptly. His girlfriend collided with him and let out a soft yelp, blinked, and wondered if she should draw her wand from inside her jacket pocket.

"Sorry," he mumbled and gestured apologetically. "I was surprised by something." He pointed to an open-air herbalist shop across the street.

Hap took small paper pouches tied off with string out of a basket far too large for him and placed them in the labeled wooden shelves facing the street—herbs, apparently, based on the shop sign. Although the ferret wore his ubiquitous red top hat, an appropriately sized apron covered his vest and chest. The shop name, The Happy Mandrake, was stenciled onto the apron in stylized script.

Raine jogged across the street and her friends fell in behind her. "Hap?"

He turned and gave them a toothy smile. It was too bad it always looked sinister when he did it. "Greetings, salutations, and hello, young ladies and gentlemen." He bowed and set his basket down. "It's always pleasant to see you all, especially on a fine day such as today." He gestured with a clawed hand toward a shelf labeled *marshmallow root*. "And not simply any day. There's a sale today. Ten percent off." His dark, beady eyes focused on Evie. "It's truly wonderful for healing potions or even non-magical preparations. High-quality stuff. Highest ever? No, that wouldn't be the truth, but the best you'll get for the price in Ruby Falls. I'd bet my hat and tail on it."

Evie waved her hands vaguely in front of her. "I'm sorry. I have more marshmallow root right now than I know what to do with."

"Of course." Hap gestured at a different shelf. "I have many fine goods. High quality too."

Cameron frowned. "What happened? I thought you were a delivery man...uh, delivery ferret." He folded his arms over his chest. "Did you get fired?"

Raine frowned at him, and he shrugged in response.

"No, my good wolf," the ferret replied, his voice full of good humor. "I was neither fired, let go, nor released from my source of previous employment. I parted from my employers rather amicably, and their willingness to speak of the high quality of my work got me a job here."

"Which is what exactly?" Raine asked and her gaze flicked to the wizened potions witch who puttered around a cauldron positioned deeper inside the shop.

"Why, young lady, I'm an apprentice herbalist." He smiled.

"An apprentice herbalist?" She blinked a few times. "But can you..." She rubbed the back of her neck. "You can't do magic, right?" She glanced at Evie, who shrugged, her expression confused.

"Ah!" He fumbled in the basket to retrieve a few more herbal packets to place in the shelves. "I see the source of confusion, especially since we're here in Ruby Falls, this magical place." He continued his work as he talked. "I'm training to do exactly what I said—become a herbalist. I'm not trying to become a potions master for the very reason you point out. I might be a creature of magic, but alas, I can't do magic. There are many, many useful things one can concoct with herbs when one has the appropriate knowledge."

Evie nodded. "That's true. My family had me practice with regular herbal preparations before my magic came in. Most of the principles of magical potions making simply build on the essence of ingredients. It's not like they are totally random or separate."

"Exactly, correct, and thorough," Hap declared. He spread his paws to the side and his whiskers twitched with excitement. "I thought about trying to become a pharmacist, but the few times I've visited non-magical cities have been difficult." He made a few popping sounds with his mouth. "Nothing is sized for me, even though I'm larger than a normal ferret. I don't understand it, frankly. I see plenty of dogs around. You'd think the humans would consider them."

Cameron chuckled. "Most of those dogs can't talk. They aren't...like you."

"I didn't realize that." The creature blinked a few times and seemed to think this through. "And I thought they were merely being rude to me because I was a ferret." He shrugged. "No matter. The point is, you kids helped me realize something important."

"What's that?" Raine asked.

"That while I constantly told myself I was living for the future, I was always actually living for today. And, of course, as an unusual creature, I have a responsibility of sorts to do well." Hap arranged the last few herbal packets to his satisfaction. "Get rich quick sounds good, but it fails for most people—which is why I didn't get rich quickly and always had trouble with creatures with dubious moral and ethical standards."

The ferret gestured to the group. "But you kids...you saved me, more than once, when you didn't have to. And I thought to myself, 'You know what, Hap? These young men and women go to this elite magic school and have so many special abilities. They didn't have to help you, but they did because they want the world to be a better place.'" He shook a tiny finger. "And that's what really made me think about what I want to do and how I want to do it. I'd already found an honest job, but what I really needed was an honest trade, something with a future."

Sara smiled. "So you went around looking for a job that would train you?"

"Something like that indeed, young lady." He adjusted the brim of his hat to a somewhat jaunty angle. "People like people who help other people. I think they will like a ferret who helps other people and being a herbalist is one way to do that. I thought about trying to become a police officer, but alas, my small size makes that difficult, impractical, and troublesome."

William glanced at Raine before he stepped forward, a suspicious look on his face. "And you don't have any more trouble with the Red Coat Society?"

Hap scoffed. "Those whiskered hooligans?" He gasped in surprise. "This must be the first time you've come to the kemana since school started, isn't it?"

The kids nodded.

"There is no more Red Coat Society in Ruby Falls," he explained. "They got too big for their coats and had too many run-ins with the local police. The result was they were told they had to leave the kemana and never come back, or they would end up in big trouble involving small rooms—and I mean small rooms for willen." He gave a feral grin. "So the entire group of them up and left. All that bad history I had with them is no longer a problem. That made it even easier to find my current job. Everything's coming up roses for Horatius A. Pierce."

The witch inside the shop crooked a finger, a soft smile on her face. Hap waved. "Sorry, but I have work to do. Thank you again, young ladies, young men, and I encourage you to come to this shop for all your herbal needs." He scurried off, the basket in hand.

Raine smiled. "That's actually refreshing."

"Refreshing?" Cameron raised an eyebrow that seemed to include both amusement and a challenge.

"Yes." She shrugged. "We're preparing for the future, but we're not the only ones. Also, it's good to be reminded of how helping people isn't always about fighting bad guys. Sometimes, it's about helping other people reach their potential—furry or otherwise."

William, Philip, and Cameron all wore serious looks and nodded. She smiled, as did Sara and Evie. Everyone had grown in their own ways because they had other people to lean on. No matter what happened after the end of their time at the School of Necessary Magic, they had shared experiences—both good and bad—and had helped each other grow.

"Let's go to Bubble & Fizz," Evie suggested quietly. "It'll be like old times."

William snickered. "Old times?"

"We don't go there much anymore." She shrugged. "I do understand why though. Something about it seems like…I don't know how to put it."

"It felt like the place we needed to be when we were younger," Cameron said and stared off into the distance. "Some places are like that. But I wouldn't mind a visit for old time's sake." He looked at Raine and she smiled.

"It's fine by me, too."

The shifter took her arm to guide her.

CHAPTER EIGHT

One Bubble & Fizz trip and a few more shops later, the students made their way down the street on their way out of the kemana. They chatted lightly about their various meal choices and how some things would never change, such as certain opinions of pineapple on pizza.

Sara laughed. "I feel like such an old woman."

"You don't look like one," Philip said with a grin. "I protest that statement very forcefully."

She rolled her eyes. "I like the compliments, but don't lay it on too thick."

Evie looked concerned. "Why do you feel like an old woman?"

"I remember what it was like to go to the old B & F as a freshman and gobble so much junk food. Now, it's barely a few years later, and I'm like, 'Ugh. There is such a thing as too much chocolate.'"

The other girls laughed.

Cameron nodded. "I know what you mean."

"We don't have to order that kind of thing," William said.

"We don't." The kitsune exhaled a long, wistful sigh. "But it's simply not the same. It was the whole collective experience, and it depended a lot on the junk food."

"I get it. It seemed way cooler when we were younger."

"Nothing stays the same," Raine said. "Maybe this is our version of senioritis? But I think change is a good thing. Life would be very boring otherwise. I think about that all the time. What if there was nothing new to learn? Even thinking that scares me."

Sara shook her head and her smile returned. "Of course, the Library Queen would be afraid of something like that."

She laughed. "I'm only a library princess this semester."

"Whatever you tell yourself to justify your addiction, Your Highness." The other girl mock-bowed. "All hail the Once and Forever Library Queen."

A beautiful woman with long brown hair that cascaded to the small of her back stood near a street corner. She smiled and chatted to a haggard-looking Light Elf. Her pristine white robe stood out among the more muted colors of the nearby buildings and street. Even the wand holster on her belt was white. A small silver pendant hung around her neck.

Something about the complicated geometric pattern inscribed in the oval pendant seemed vaguely familiar to Raine, but she couldn't immediately identify it. Perhaps that was why she stared at it for as long as she did. The elf mumbled something and walked away.

The woman offered him a final nod and strolled toward Raine. "Hello."

She blinked and her cheeks heated when she realized she'd been staring. "Hello. Um, sorry, I didn't mean to stare."

"Staring is merely an admission of interest." The stranger still smiled easily. "And is it so wrong to be interested in others?"

"No, I guess not." She shrugged.

"You have the look of students." The woman glanced at each student. "I'm new here, but I assume you're from the School of Necessary Magic?"

Cameron nodded. Raine could tell he tried not to frown as he said, "Yes. We're seniors."

The woman sighed wistfully and looked aside for a moment. "Such wonderful memories, magic school."

"You went to our school?" Raine asked. Now that she was closer, she could sense the moderate magic emitted by the pendant.

The stranger shook her head. "No, no. I went to a different, smaller school. The Orono Academy for Arcane Studies. It's in Maine."

"Really?" She smiled. "We did a project with students and professors from there over the summer on New Firefly Island."

The woman gasped and her mouth curled in a warm smile. "I heard about that. To think a mallaoch would be off the coast of Maine. We used to joke about all the sea monsters we thought were hiding near the state. Some even were, but still…" She shook her head. "Something so special and grand." She frowned. "How rude of me. I haven't introduced myself." She extended a slender hand. "I'm Cina."

Raine took the hand and shook it. "Raine Campbell. And this is Cameron, Evie, William, Philip, and Sara." She nodded to each of her friends in turn.

"It's wonderful to meet you all." Cina's smile was so warm it was almost soothing. "I was actually in the first class at OAAS after the gates began to open when it changed from a school where magicals were to an actual magical school."

"That must have been nice," she replied. The woman didn't look that much older than them—her early twenties at most—but she had long since adjusted to the reality that it was difficult to judge the age of any magical by their appearance, even if they weren't gnomes.

"I don't know if it's nicer than going to a magical school now." Cina's smile faltered. "Despite all the troubles in the world, the open return of magic is the open return of wonder, and I look forward to a bright future. I sometimes think older witches like myself are tainted by memories of what it meant to spend years in a world that did everything it could to insist magic wasn't real."

Cameron shrugged. "I don't know if that was a bad thing. There is considerable trouble now."

"Because people hid things for so long." Cina shook her head. "If there had been honesty from the beginning, we could have a wonderful age of magical and non-magical living side-by-side, even with the more limited magical energy." She sighed. "Oh, I apologize. I can get so stuck in my musings at times." She gestured to the group of friends. "And with students like you leading the way, there's nothing but hope for the future. Once magic truly becomes integrated into Earth, it'll be a golden age."

"I hope so." Raine couldn't tear her gaze off the pendant. The more she saw it, the more familiar it looked, but not being able to place it was a real distraction. "That's a beautiful pendant."

The woman fingered the pendant. "It's an artifact if you couldn't already tell. Nothing all that impressive, but it's been in my family for generations." She uttered a quiet little chuckle. "Since I like you all so much, I'll even let you in on a little semi-secret."

"What's that?" Sara asked, a hint of suspicion in her voice.

Raine knew what she thought. Cina wouldn't be the first woman to approach them and offer them an alleged ancient artifact in exchange for some ridiculous price. They never took the bait. After all, even if someone wandered Ruby Falls with an ancient artifact, it wasn't like they would actually sell it to a random group of teenagers.

"Some people in my family claim it's very ancient." She lowered her hand from the pendant. "Thousands of years old, maybe even tens of thousands. My grandmother used to say it was made the last time the gates were open."

"Woah," Philip said and stepped forward, a curious look on his face. "There are spells you can use to test for that, though, right?"

"Not all are reliable." Cina blushed. "But I'll admit another secret to you all. No one in my family has ever bothered to test it. We know it's at least a few hundred years old, but we can't confirm more than that."

"Why didn't you test it?" The wizard frowned, openly confused.

"Because sometimes, the mystery is more attractive than the answer." She tapped the pendant. "Don't you think?"

Cameron laughed. "You don't know Raine." He grinned at her when she glared at him. "She can't stand unsolved mysteries. If there's a clue out there, she'll chase it to the bitter end."

Everyone else chuckled.

Cina tilted her head and her gaze turned appraising. "Would you say that's accurate?"

Raine shrugged. "I suppose. I don't like leaving mysteries unsolved, and I don't like leaving people who need help."

"How wonderful. So many young people, even magicals, are focused on the wrong things." The woman sighed. "They forget they have a power that billions on this planet don't, and they should use that to make the world a better place."

"I agree. We all do." Raine narrowed her eyes on the pendant. "I think I've seen this pattern before. What does it mean?"

Cina gave her a tight smile, a hint of mischief in her eyes. "After what Cameron just told me, I think I don't want to tell you."

"You don't? Why?"

"Because I think it'll be interesting for me to see if you can find it out." She waved cheerfully. "And I must apologize, but I have an appointment. Even though I'm only visiting Ruby Falls, I'll be here for a while. Once you've solved the mystery, track me down, Raine."

She sighed, frustrated to be denied the immediate answer. "And where are you staying?"

"Another mystery you'll need to solve." Her warm smile persisted as she walked away.

"That was kind of weird," Cameron muttered.

"Better than a crazy chaos witch, dude," Philip pointed out.

"That's a pretty low standard."

Raine frowned. "It really is driving me crazy. I know I've seen that symbol." She shook her head. "I wish she had simply told me."

Sara grinned. "It'll probably be disappointing. After all, how special could it be if she wears it out in public, especially in a robe like that? It's like she's trying to attract attention."

"What did she say she did again?" William frowned as he tried to recall the full conversation.

"She didn't," Raine said. "Another mystery."

Cameron snickered. "It's not a mystery simply because you didn't ask, but let's get going. Don't you have FBI scenario reports you need to turn into Agent Connor?"

She grimaced. "Oh, yeah. I'd almost forgotten." She glanced at the half-Ifrit.

"I did mine yesterday," he responded.

"I was really engrossed in another ancient beasts book at the library. Now I remember why I had to cut back. Ugh."

Raine spared one last glance at the departing Cina who

was still visible in the distance. Perhaps mystery was what lay at the heart of all magic, which in the end, involved people trying to bend the universe to their will for whatever reasons, noble or evil. Every new day at school and every new encounter at the kemana only reinforced the truth that she had barely begun to understand all the mysteries of magic.

Her heart rate kicked up at the thought. It was excitement, not fear. There was still so much to learn.

CHAPTER NINE

Adrien licked his lips and his heart pounded. As the days had bled into weeks at the school and the Cardinals had played their first few matches, careful tactics had rewarded them with victory. But all those opponents were distant to his concerns, mere obstacles in the journey.

Today's match was different. For the first time in his Louper career, he had to face an actual friend, Finn, and he hoped for a good battle. Not doing everything he could to win against him would be an insult to them both, as he'd already explained to the rest of the team.

"Orono's simply another stop on our way to victory," he announced. "We don't need to have a perfect season to win the championship, but I'd strongly prefer it. So, let's hurry and get across these asteroids."

The current Cardinals line-up marched across the rocky, dusty surface of what appeared to be a stationary asteroid floating in the middle of nowhere. the Light Elf walked in front with Hilda, Carlos, Jackson, and Dennis behind him. A star-filled sky surrounded them on all sides with the occasional flash in the distance, but otherwise, there was nothing but dozens of hunks of space debris hanging in nothingness. The teams' attempts to track the token had failed so far.

The captain's stomach lurched when he looked down. There was nothing below them but more stars, not even asteroids. False Louper reality didn't always bother him. He took pride in understanding that no matter what it felt like it, nothing around him was real, but his brain betrayed him in this match. He took a deep breath to settle his stomach.

The team approached the edge of the rocky sphere. Burst spells launched them to the next. They might look like they were in space, but the gravitational pull felt similar to Earth. Whether they were actually pulled down was a relative question. He didn't care about the accuracy of physics, only about the consistency and how his team might respond. Unless the gravity suddenly changed, they wouldn't have to worry unless they missed their landings.

A small planet materialized in the distance as the team jumped to their destination asteroid. It resembled a tiny Mercury, about ten yards in diameter. Any doubt he had about what it was supposed to represent was quashed by the presence of the flashing and rotating astrological symbol for Mercury hovering about the north pole.

Shadows coalesced on the surface into four-armed forms. Adrien summoned a sword and rushed toward one of the shadow warriors. He sliced it in half with a deft swing, and it disappeared. A barrage of orbs from his teammates eliminated the other monsters.

He waited for about fifteen seconds for more creatures

to attack before he gestured to Mercury. A couple more jumps took them close to the planet. The team arrived on the nearest asteroid and studied the larger sphere with suspicion. Its presence had to mean something, but they weren't sure what. Additional asteroid paths led away in different directions.

The elf frowned. Mercury wasn't rotating, but there weren't any obvious unusual patterns or places with which to interact.

"What now?" Dennis asked, his wand at the ready. His gaze scrutinized their destination as he looked for the opposing team.

The captain considered the situation for a few seconds before he raised his hand and chanted a revelation spell. A bright, glowing arrow appeared above the pole, pointing in the direction of one of the asteroid paths.

"I think we follow the arrow." Adrien summoned a sword. "But keep your shields ready. Mercury appeared out of nowhere, which means we can't actually see everything, and if we're starting there, Orono is probably starting out near an outer planet and working their way in. The weak monsters probably mean there's some other twist to this match."

Hilda narrowed her eyes and peered into the distance. She raised her wand and cast a quick telescopic vision spell. "Even with help, nothing looks closer."

"All the more reason to be careful." He lowered his hands and pointed at the surface of the asteroid. His burst sent him to the top of the planet ahead and his skin tingled as he passed through the symbol. Without hesitation, he burst again to the start of the new asteroid path.

Dennis followed him and landed on the side of Mercury but didn't fall. He blinked a few times and looked down as his face tightened. "This is so weird. On the asteroid, down felt like...well, down, but here, down feels like toward the center."

"It wouldn't be Louper without a challenge," Adrien called as he landed on the next chunk of rock. He waved. "Let's hurry. I want to stay together as a team."

His teammate walked to the pole. "Look at me, I'm the King of Mercury."

"Please join me, Your Majesty," the elf yelled and rolled his eyes.

Dennis grinned and a quick burst brought him alongside the captain. Hilda and Carlos joined him seconds later.

The team continued in this way and the path brought them to Venus and additional trails. More shadow monsters appeared, but they dispatched them with little difficulty. Earth wasn't that far away, followed by Mars and soon, Adrien stood on top of the tiny red planet, his arms folded.

"We've traversed four planets. Assuming Orono started at either Neptune or Pluto, they might be very, very close." The captain narrowed his eyes before he jumped to the start of the next path. "Everyone needs to be careful. I can't sub you out if you're eliminated."

The team gathered and followed him almost as a simultaneous unit. Their bounding trip took them to a half-dozen asteroids before a wide circular island of black stone appeared. About fifty yards across, it contained a fountain of blue-white flames in the center. While it was too smooth and regular to be called an asteroid in

Adrien's mind, a dozen space trails led away from the rocky island.

He threw a fist up, and everyone stopped. "This is different."

"The token's probably in the flames," Dennis suggested. He raised his wand and cast a quick tracking spell, but the orb fizzled. He shrugged. "They might have blocked it."

The elf attempted a revelation spell. Two arrows appeared but pointed inward. He looked across at the corresponding asteroid paths.

"What does that mean?" Hilda asked with a frown.

He frowned. "I'm not sure. It might mean there is more than one way to get there, or they have a new puzzle that requires people in different places, but that wouldn't be consistent with what the league said they had planned for this year. Let's get on the island and figure it out from there."

The Cardinals all burst to the island and landed at the edge. Something shimmered in the distance on the other side.

"Move!" Adrien yelled and darted forward. "Break formation!"

Hilda, Carlos, and Jackson sprinted ahead in different directions. Dennis hesitated for a few seconds.

Five voices shouted an incantation at the same time. Orono's team appeared out of nowhere about twenty yards away, their wands pointed. Five dark orbs erupted from the tips and rocketed into the ground near the Cardinals.

The entire island shuddered. Huge cracks slivered out from the point of impact. Dennis fell to his knees and lost his grip on his wand. A moment later, a loud groan provided yet another reminder that they weren't in space. The edge of the island ripped away and tumbled into the star-filled void. The wand slid with it and fell, twirling as it did so.

The boy yelled and clambered to safety. Without a wand, he had no choice but to jump rather than burst and stretched his long fingers in desperation. A single hand found purchase on the edge.

Adrien hurled a few slime spells toward the opposing team, hoping to distract them. "Jackson, help Dennis."

"But he doesn't have his wand," the player said with a shrug.

"I can still sub him out."

Hilda and Carlos added their own slime to his efforts without questioning the strategy. The enemy team scattered, but they hadn't tried any new spells, which was cause for concern.

Understanding dawned on Jackson's face, and he raced toward his teammate, who struggled to pull himself up. The elf made a mental note to increase non-magical strength training for the team.

He smiled when a massive glob of viscous gunk caught one of the Orono players. The now-blinded wizard had been too close to the edge, stumbled over, and yelled as he fell. Finn's large silhouette stood on the inside of the team's formation, which placed him closer to the flames at the center of the island, but his expression remained unreadable at the distance.

The opposition team all shouted the same spell as before to launch another volley of orbs. It took Adrien a moment to realize they hadn't aimed at the bulk of his team but instead, at the edge of the island. Jackson had just reached over to grasp Dennis when the spell struck. Both wizards spiraled toward the stars.

The captain hissed in irritation and released a volley of fireballs. They might not blind the other team, but they would limit their movement more and force them to refresh their shields. He raised a few stone barriers from the island as he darted from one place to another, and the rocky protection absorbed the quick blasts directed at him in response. Hilda and Carlos spread out behind him and took position behind the shields. Three of the Orono players spun away from Finn and launched orbs that kicked up considerable dust but didn't otherwise dent the Cardinals' fortifications.

"What's Finn doing?" the elf mumbled. A light orb whizzed overhead.

The large Orono player jogged directly toward the flame, his head slightly raised. Adrien mimicked his movement and caught sight of a glint of metal in the flames. His eyes widened.

"The arrows aren't pointing toward other paths," he shouted to his team. "They are pointing at the token. I need you to cover me."

"We'll keep them down," Hilda said. She chanted quickly and popped up to fire a pulsating orb. It careened toward the Orono players and exploded in a bright flash and shower of sparks. Carlos followed up with a few rapid blinding spells of his own.

The Light Elf surged from his cover and raced toward the flames, his gaze locked on the glint of the coin. He layered a few more shields over himself before he summoned a sword and cast another burst spell. Finn didn't attack and, instead, burst up himself. A shimmering translucent blade extended from his wand. Both boys focused their trajectory on the token. The flames licked at Adrien but didn't strain his shield, a distraction rather than a true obstacle.

The opposing player's sword met his with a resounding thunk, and the blades crossed. They plummeted into the bright flames. The elf snaked his hand out and snatched the prize as they both landed hard with similar grunts.

"Not good enough, bro," Finn yelled. "Sorry, but I have to take this for my team." He scrambled to his feet and searched for the coin.

Adrien stood and grinned as he held the token up. It was another victory for the Cardinals.

CHAPTER TEN

Raine smiled at Evie as they both inspected their cauldrons for cracks. "I always love a new unit, don't you? New unit means new potion."

She'd been sad that it was only the Trouble Squad girls in the potions section that semester, but as the weeks passed, she'd adjusted to the idea. It wasn't like she had a huge amount of time to talk to her friends during class, but somehow, discussing everything that happened was always more interesting if they shared the same section, despite the same material being covered in the different classes.

The other girl nodded, eagerness written on her face. "I wonder what it is. Professor Fowler won't give us any hints. I bet it's something very fun. That's why she wanted to surprise us with it. I can't wait."

Sara eyed her cauldron with a frown where she sat on the other side of Raine. "It's a senior-level potion. Even if it's fun, it'll be complicated. That means more things to go wrong."

Evie shook her head. "It means more things can go right."

Raine flipped over a small piece of paper on her table. "This doesn't make any sense. A calming potion? Why would we study that again?"

Evie checked hers. "A cloud potion? Why are we studying something like that at all, and why would mine be different than yours?" She flipped it over again. Typically, when Professor Fowler gave them recipes face down, she didn't want them getting ahead of themselves.

"I'm sure she has a good reason. Maybe we'll do some sort of technique review. I'm not as excited about that, but she knows what she's doing."

The girls, along with the background murmur of the rest of the class, fell silent as Professor Fowler strolled in and walked toward her cauldron at the front of the class. She cleared her throat and waited until she had everyone's full attention. "This is the start of a new unit for one of our more complicated potions, but one you will continue to use throughout the rest of your life, regardless of what path you follow."

Evie's mouth parted, and she leaned forward, eager to receive new potions wisdom.

The professor smiled. "Today, class, we'll start learning how to brew a proper scouring potion."

A collective groan swept the classroom. Only Evie still seemed interested.

Raine took a deep breath and nodded while she tried to summon her enthusiasm once again. Yes, a glorified cleaning potion wasn't exactly the most exciting thing she had ever learned, but it was time they took responsibility for something critically important to potion making—maintaining their cauldrons.

Professor Fowler chuckled, not a trace of offense or disappointment on her face. "Oh, I understand how this might sound, especially since it's so complicated. I understand the attraction of impressive rewards for impressive efforts."

Malcolm raised his hand in the corner. "Why is it so complicated? I don't understand why we can't make a normal cleaning or restoration potion?"

"Does anyone care to answer?" The witch's gaze drifted to Evie. "Someone who remembered me explaining this before."

The class laughed, and the boy winced. There was a price attached to not paying attention.

"Because it's not only a matter of cleaning off old liquid or particles," Evie explained, her voice filled with complete confidence. "It also has to clean off the residual magic and enchantments that linger in the cauldron to eliminate any chance of cross-reaction."

The professor nodded and looked pleased. "Exactly. Normally, the basic construction of the cauldrons along with the spells that go into their creation help cut down on too much residual magical lingering, but constant use still raises the risk of interactions. The scouring potion isn't a mere cleaning potion, but one combined with general suppression and active anti-magic elements. It's rather impressive when you think about it. It's not as exciting as some of the potions I've taught you, but it's one that's reflective of many of the core techniques you have learned and involves many ingredients you've worked with in the past. Now, there is a huge list of ingredients and a number of preparation steps." A few scattered groans met this pronouncement. "But," she continued, "we won't worry about that today. You'll study the recipe, and we'll begin the multi-day brewing process in the next class session."

Hope crept onto the faces of some of the students. They had long since learned that multi-day lessons tended to be less stressful overall.

"What will we do today, then?" Raine asked. She gestured to a tray of herbs and a rack of liquid-filled vials. "What's all this for? We're brewing, right?"

"We'll learn by experience what happens when you don't use a scouring potion." Professor Fowler pointed at her cauldron. "Every cauldron in this room has been specially prepared as a lesson. A fun little project I set up in the summer to demonstrate what can go wrong if you don't properly and regularly scour your equipment. I save it for the senior year because there's no point in the demonstration until you're ready for the potion." She raised her hand to her mouth and coughed into it. "Now, I must insist you all shield yourselves for maximum safety."

Evie's interested smile remained as she raised her wand to summon a powerful shield. Raine, along with most students, grimaced. She picked her wand up to cast her own shield and her stomach knotted. The anticipation could be worse than the actual event.

"Yes. We're definitely brewing, but not for the reason you might have thought." The professor clapped twice. "All right, students, fill your cauldrons halfway and bring them to boil. It's time to see the price of laziness. If you turn over the recipes on your desk, you'll find they're all different because they're each intended to demonstrate a different failure. Let's get started. If you all follow the recipes as written, we shouldn't see our first failure for about twenty minutes."

Malcolm's equipment was the first victim. He had barely finished adding powdered tourmaline when his cauldron began frosting over.

"Huh?" The boy backed away with a frown.

"Everyone stop," Professor Fowler commanded. She pointed at his result. The frost thickened and spread until the entire object was covered. "Clear some of it off."

He strengthened his shield before he wiped a little of the frost away to reveal that the metal beneath had changed to ice. "Won't it melt?" he asked dubiously and blinked several times.

She nodded. "Yes. I would stop your flame." She smiled and pointed to Juniper's cauldron in the corner. "Ah, I hadn't expected that yet either."

Everyone turned to look and Juniper jerked her head toward her cauldron. She'd been fixated on Malcolm's and had almost forgotten hers. Small tentacles writhed inside and poked up from the center of the dark liquid. The girl paled and backed away.

Professor Fowler clucked her tongue. "Oh, don't worry. They're really quite harmless. In this case, I would keep the heat on until they sink back into the liquid."

The student stared nervously at the still-writhing

appendages from what should have been an ordinary potion. "Okay."

The witch shook a finger at the class. "This is why it's ever so important to scour properly. Potion making is only predictable when you control all the conditions, and the state of your cauldron is one of the major factors." She smiled at Evie. "Why don't you add your next ingredient? Do you have any idea of what might happen?"

Evie nodded. "It's not really that bad."

"Then show the class."

She picked up a vial containing an ochre liquid and emptied it into the bubbling cauldron before she pulled her hand back and stepped away. The liquid frothed and the colors shifted between different shades of light and dark.

Raine glanced from her friend to the potion. Evie didn't look particularly concerned, which suggested it wouldn't blow up or breed any strange monsters.

A single mournful note issued from the cauldron, then a high note. The color changes increased speed, each shift now accompanied by a clear musical note. The strange song continued for a good minute and sometimes approached a semi-coherent melody before the liquid turned gray and the sound ceased.

"Entertaining," the professor said. "But wasteful. All the ingredients used thus far aren't recoverable, but admittedly, that failure is far less disturbing and dangerous than some of the others."

Sara tilted her head and stared into her cauldron. All her liquid had vanished and she scowled. "Isn't this only us making the wrong potion?"

"In a sense, yes. I'm glad you realize that, but the

effects you notice, even if you find them interesting, can be accomplished in a far more efficient way with a traditional potion-making recipe." She smiled. "Please note, though, that I've prepared these cauldrons and your suggested recipe carefully to elicit them. In a normal circumstance, the result would be more random. I merely wanted to demonstrate some of the things that might occur."

Another student's cauldron shattered into hundreds of tiny pieces with an explosive pop. The stench of rotting fish arose from another. Professor Fowler quickly created an air bubble around it, her point made. Fire, flower petals, and a cauldron disappearing completely defined the next few incidents.

"While you might have understood the importance of scouring before, I hope you have all now thoroughly internalized it by experiencing it." She nodded to the class.

Raine took a deep breath as the woman smiled at her. It was her turn.

"Add your next ingredient, please," the professor ordered.

She picked up a small orange petal, held it high above her cauldron, and released it quickly before she jerked her hand back. The petal floated gently toward the bubbling luminescent green liquid. It landed on the surface and sizzled as it sank into the thick magical soup.

The brew crackled and pink smoke consumed the cauldron. She backed away, her wand at the ready, but the smoke settled and dissipated. The cauldron was gone, replaced by a full-sized chocolate rabbit.

"A chocolate bunny?" Her tone sounded a little more

high-pitched than normal, and she cleared her throat hastily.

Professor Fowler raised an eyebrow. "Hmm. That's not even what I expected. This particular side-effect tends to produce food but usually, something not so sweet. Don't try to eat it, though. It'll revert to a cauldron in a few minutes."

Raine stared at the chocolate and shook her head. She'd always known scouring was important but not how much. While a part of her still hated the idea of the effort required, she would never take it for granted again.

CHAPTER ELEVEN

It was her turn to choose the movie, and Raine's grin was so wide she could eat the world as she settled on one of the couches in the movie room, a DVD case in hand. Cameron smiled at her and turned to stare longingly at a bag of barbecue chips. Philip had the bag open and was dumping them into a wide green bowl that rested on the table along with the other snacks.

Sara looked at her. "You're in a good mood."

Cameron dragged his gaze from temptation to look at Raine. "Yeah. What's with the all smiles? What movie did you choose? It's not like you bring things we don't like, so this can't be some big joke."

She lifted the DVD case. "I didn't pick it. That's why I'm smiling."

"Uh, I didn't pick it." The shifter looked at Sara but she shook her head. He then glanced at Evie, and she shrugged. Adrien sipped on a cup of water, an amused look in his eyes. William and Philip remained far more focused on the snacks than the discussion.

Raine stood, the huge grin cemented in place. "Madelyn picked it. She finally agreed to come."

"Really?" Cameron asked, his voice filled with surprise. "What changed?"

"Time, I think." She crossed to the DVD player and set the case on top of it. "I've asked her several times since the start of the semester. It's not like I've harassed her or anything, but I do see her in the library. I rearranged my schedule a little so I could have more library time and talk to her more. Earlier this morning, I was there and she was reading a book on the history of movies. It was the perfect opening, so I asked her, and she agreed."

Sara smiled. "That's great. What movie did she choose? Is it something we've seen before? You didn't have time to run to town or the kemana."

"*Koyaanisqatsi*," Raine replied and her tongue stumbled over the title. "I got lucky. Head Librarian Decker already had a copy. He said it was 'very interesting.'"

"What's it about?" Her boyfriend looked distinctly uneasy.

"I'm not sure. When I asked him that, he told me he thought it would be better if we watched it without 'normal preconceptions.'" She tapped the DVD case. "And this case only has the movie inside. It doesn't have any labels or anything."

Philip filled a smaller paper bowl with chips before he moved toward Sara. "I have a feeling we'll regret this."

"We can't say anything," Raine said, her eyes pleading. "No matter what we think of the movie. Madelyn chose it. If we make her feel bad about it, she might never come back."

He sighed. "Understood. I won't say anything even if this is the suckiest one I've ever seen."

The other students all nodded their affirmation, determination on their faces. There were worse sacrifices for friendship than watching bad movies, and they'd all brought at least one that someone in the group didn't like.

A light knock sounded the door. She took a deep breath and headed over there. "Here we go." She opened it. Madelyn stood on the other side, her hands folded in front of her as she looked down.

Raine gestured to an empty seat on the couch. "Welcome to movie night, Madelyn. We have snacks on the table—popcorn, chips, candy, soda, that kind of thing. Now that the guest of honor has arrived, we can get started."

The Coral Elf crept into the room, her eyes still downcast. "T-thank you for inviting me, Raine." She walked the entire way to her seat without raising her head and only finally looked up to focus on the TV. "I hope you like the movie."

Raine closed the door and hurried over to the DVD player. She slipped the disc in, surprised when only a single underlined menu option came up, the movie title in yellow. Quickly, she pressed start and headed back to her seat.

Low music played. Red lines expanded into the letters of the title. Deep male voices joined the electronic music and chanted slowly in an unknown language. The camera panned out to reveal pictographs on a canyon wall of tall, dark figures. The slow pan continued and blended into an image of a huge fire. A slow transition followed to reveal that the fire was the rocket thrust from a Saturn V rocket. The music remained unchanged and repetitive—low, deep music matched with equally low, deep voices. Slow pacing extended the length of the rocket launch until that scene gave way to an aerial view of desert canyons.

"So, will there be a narration or something?" Philip asked. "I'm not sure what's going on." He winced as everyone else gave him a dirty look.

Madelyn stared at the television, her mouth parted and her differently colored eyes wide with interest. Raine had never seen her look so fascinated.

The wizard's hope for narration or at least a basic explanation seemed misplaced. Footage of waves and clouds filled the next section and haunting music playing the entire time. They gave way to choppy water and rows and rows of planted flowers and rocks.

"Intriguing," Adrien murmured with an approving nod. "Very intriguing."

"It is that," Philip said quietly. He winced as Sara elbowed him.

Whatever charms the film possessed, a clear story or defined characters were not among them. The tapestry of images and haunting music continued to mix the natural world and technological—from the grand, such as a dam, to the horrifying in the infamously iconic mushroom cloud that accompanied a nuclear weapon explosion. Footage of large jets and cars streaming along roads like trails of ants was followed by that of older military vehicles, tanks from the Soviet Union, and an aircraft carrier.

Slow-motion and time-lapse shots began to dominate visual explorations of clouds and the destruction of decaying apartment buildings. The ruination transitioned to sunset on glass and a busy city with people living and working in factories, eating, or walking. There was a noticeable increase in the tempo of the music along with the frequency of cuts from shot to shot.

Raine could honestly say she'd never seen anything like it.

———

No one spoke as the film continued through increasing numbers of scenes that depicted technological human civilization, both high and low. The dialog-free minutes continued to pass until the final scenes. Another rocket lifted off, followed by more pictographs. The title reappeared with a definition below and defined it as a Hopi word meaning crazy life, life in turmoil, life out of balance, life disintegrating, or a state of life that calls for another way of living.

Madelyn frowned as the movie cut back to the menu. "There was more. I wonder why it was cut."

"More?" Philip squeaked.

She nodded. "There should be translations of some of the chanting. They were Hopi prophecies."

"Hopi? Like the tribe? Prophecies?" Cameron asked. "And like the Seers?"

The Coral Elf shrugged. "I don't know. It mostly implies that people should be careful about what they take from the land." She smiled with uncharacteristic confidence. "I don't know if that's even real, though. They could have simply put them in the movie. I haven't looked it up to confirm it."

"Is it totally weird that it made more sense to me as it went on?" Philip asked.

Adrien shook his head. "No, despite the lack of dialog, the depicted narrative purpose was straightforward. The rise of technological civilization and its influence on both this planet and humanity. It's an interesting film."

Sara nodded. "Once I realized there was no big plot coming, it was easier to simply absorb the images."

Raine looked at Madelyn. "I wonder if there's a film that explores what it's like to live on the two worlds now with technology and magic."

The girl looked at her hands in her lap. "I think they need more time to figure out what it means, at least for Earth. Oricerans could make one." There was more confidence in her voice than normal.

William scarfed a few chips. "Madelyn, I agree with everyone else. I got it, I think, but I wonder why you picked this film. We all choose our films for different reasons. Sometimes for fun, sometimes to feel something. This was interesting, but it's very different than the kind of thing we normally watch."

She rubbed her wrist. "Head Librarian Decker suggested it to me. He said I would find it interesting. I did, but I also liked it for a different reason." She blushed, the redness vivid on her pale cheeks.

"What's that?" Raine offered the girl a comforting smile.

"I didn't understand the language, and it's so low and repetitive in those parts that it's easy to think of as music. I could concentrate on the images and absorb the meaning of what I saw. I like the idea of communication without words." She sighed. "I don't know. I think a lot about myself and my own words—if I can even trust them myself because I'm not real. The movie's nothing but experiences. It feels more real to me without words. I still don't know who I am, and it makes me question myself every day."

Raine shook her head, stood, and walked over to take a seat beside her. "You're real, Madelyn."

Cameron nodded, a slight frown on his face. "You're here, right now, watching a weird art movie. How much more real can you get?"

"I think about it all the time. I just came into existence. No, we did—Vianna and me—before we became two." The Coral Elf lifted her hand and stared at it as if it was the oddest thing she had ever seen. "I feel, but I don't know if that's the same thing. I've found that I like movies like this or music without words, things I can experience and feel without my thoughts intruding."

She patted the elf's hand. "None of us choose where and how we will be born, and not every race on the two worlds is born the same way. You're as real as any of us, and the fact that you feel is proof of that."

Sara nodded firmly. "You're our friend, and you're definitely not an imaginary friend."

"No fake girl would have brought a movie like that." Philip chuckled.

William looked thoughtful. "Most of us were unsure about ourselves when we started at this school. I think Raine was one of the few who had a clear vision of who she was and who she wanted to be." He glanced at her before he returned his focus to Madelyn. "Not knowing who you are is the most normal thing you could feel at a place like this. But remember, you have friends now, and we're always willing to help you."

Madelyn sniffled and teared up. She raised her sleeve to wipe her eyes. "Thank you."

Raine risked a hug, and the girl leaned into it. "William's right. You have friends now, and everything will be okay."

CHAPTER TWELVE

"Again?" Mara frowned at Xander from her couch.

He paced in front of her coffee table, his brow furrowed. "I don't see that I have another option."

"This is ill-advised." She shook her head. "You've based this on insufficient information. Even if everything Syras told you wasn't a lie, it doesn't change the fact that he could be wrong."

He stopped, looked at her, and chuckled. "You don't believe that, and I don't need a truth spell to confirm it."

She arched an eyebrow. "Oh?"

"If you didn't believe someone was coming back for me, you wouldn't try to convince me it's a waste of time to trawl the kemana." Xander headed toward the door of her cabin. "This is the only chance we have to end this."

"And how long will you keep this up? Three months? Six months? A year? What if no one ever comes?"

He forced a grin. "Then I'll spend a lot of time walking around the kemana for nothing. It's always good to develop new hobbies."

Xander strolled along the streets of Ruby Falls and his careful gaze scrutinized every new person who turned a corner. The enemy would never show themselves if he remained holed up on school grounds. The only way to end everything would be to draw them out, and that required him to expose himself where an assassin might feel comfortable using magic. That wouldn't be in Charlottesville.

In addition, he couldn't be certain, if someone did return to kill him, that they might not eschew their previous subtle tactics and try something flashier and more overt. The density of magicals in Ruby Falls increased the chance that people might be able to defend themselves against a magical attack.

Mara might not want him to risk himself, but he didn't want her to risk herself again either. He had been sloppy and allowed himself to be poisoned the first time, and now, he was determined to solve the problem with his own efforts and wand. He stopped at a corner.

A beautiful woman in a white robe crossed the street in the distance. He'd bumped into Cina a few times but didn't know much about her other than rumors that she was involved in some sort of secretive group.

That, in and of itself, didn't bother him, especially since she'd shown zero interest in talking to him other than exchanging pleasantries, and she hadn't performed any magic even close to dark magic. He suspected she was merely another in a long line of hucksters there to separate fools and their money. Being a magical didn't make one immune to being conned, especially since it was hard to force most people to agree to a truth spell.

Ruby Falls was full of secrets, many of them dangerous, but he only cared about the ones that involved dark wizard assassins. He was concerned with saving Mara, the school, and himself in that order. Everything else was a distant fourth place in his list of concerns.

Xander turned a corner and nodded politely to an Ifrit potter who worked in a tiny shop only a few yards away. He'd bought a pot from the man a few weeks before. The more money he spread around, the more people would talk about him, and that would help to draw out his enemies.

The one disadvantage of being in Ruby Falls versus Charlottesville was that the baseline level of magic was so high that simply sensing magical activity wasn't necessarily indicative of anything. The juxtaposition of a spell and the sensation of being watched was different, though.

He stopped and surveyed the area slowly. The potter stood in the distance, his palms out, and jets of flame burst forth as he fired his wares. A Kilomea stood on the street corner and spun a glowing sign to attract customers to the opening of a new restaurant. A group of pixies fluttered along in the distance. Witches, wizards, and elves filled the busy street and a few cast curious glances his way, but none stared at him with undue interest or focus.

"What did I expect?" Xander mumbled under his breath. "Someone pointing their wand at my back?" He shook his head and continued along the street toward a claustrophobia-inducing covered alley farther ahead. It was time to bait the hook more enticingly, and he turned into it.

The sensation of being watched remained, but a look over his shoulder revealed nothing. He raised his hand to his jacket and grasped his wand.

An enemy who failed before might change tactics. They might not feel compelled to ambush him in a flashy way in a street full of magicals, but a fireball in the back while he was in an alley might provide a satisfying revenge. He cast a shield spell and continued toward the other end of the narrow passage.

A voice drifted from around the corner of the front of the alleyway. "...Powell..."

He continued casually, his wand at the ready. Murmured conversation drifted to him, obviously between two people, but he couldn't make out the words. His brain had grasped his last name in the distance, the magic of basic human neurobiology. Was the enemy waiting for him at the front of the alley and following him from the back?

No more hiding. That's what he had sworn to himself and Mara. He refused to live in fear, but the longer the situation continued, the longer his new life would be on hold. All his efforts to win her back had succeeded, and he wouldn't allow anyone from the old days to take that from him. He'd earned it.

Xander jogged forward now, and his heart rate kicked up. It was time to end this farce and put his past behind him once and for all. The shadows of two people appeared at the entrance. He halted and raised his wand. The owners of the shadows stepped forward, and he lowered his arm hastily.

There were no dark wizard assassins, only Raine and Cameron walking arm in arm. The boy swung his head toward the wizard and his eyes flashed yellow as if he sensed the danger of an armed wizard ready to attack. Her breath caught and her hand went to her jacket. They both had good instincts for trouble, better than they should for magicals their age.

He uttered a rueful chuckle. While he was proud to train his students in different magical techniques, he also hoped that every lesson would be unnecessary. After what had happened with Izzie, such a desire almost seemed naïve, but some, like the FBI Trouble Squad, had found far more use for his lessons than others.

The shifter continued to stare at him, his eyes still yellow and his face tight. Xander hid his wand under the flap of his jacket. The boy wasn't only a boyfriend but a shifter protecting the woman he loved. The protective instinct wasn't something to be ignored simply because he thought he saw a friendly face.

The tension drained from Raine's face and a smile spread to replace it. "That's so weird."

Xander tried his best to be casual as he slipped his wand back into his holster. "What's weird, Raine?"

"We were just talking about you." Raine laughed. "I hope there's not some professor spell you didn't tell us about where if we say your name, you'll suddenly appear."

Cameron didn't smile. "You were expecting trouble. You had your wand out."

He shot him a practiced grin. "Expect the worst and you'll always be pleasantly surprised." He fluffed his jacket. "I got into an argument with a rather disagreeable wizard earlier today," he lied. "It's nothing serious, but I thought he had followed me, looking for trouble."

"Why not go to the police?"

"They have better things to do than worry about what are probably nothing more than empty threats." He shrugged. "But you were talking about me?"

Raine nodded. "Technically, we were talking about most of our professors. But I happen to enjoy your class the most this semester so far. You always keep things interesting."

"It's not always a fair comparison," Xander replied. "It's easy to impress students with flashy battle spells compared to lectures or something more subtle like many potions. I know I have one of the more entertaining subjects at the school. It also helps to have talented students to teach."

She smiled. "Thank you, Professor." She chuckled. "It's not all that cool to be talking about our classes on a date, now that I think about it."

Cameron grunted and shrugged. His eyes had finally returned to normal, but he had stepped forward to place himself in between her and Xander.

"I'm only glad I keep it interesting enough for you to talk about," the professor said. "I didn't mean to interrupt your date. Sorry about that."

"It's not like you were trying," she said.

The shifter stepped back and tugged on her arm. "Yes. It's not like you were trying." Suspicion dripped from his voice. He looked past the man down the alley. "Does the headmistress know about what you're doing down here?"

Xander smirked. "And what is it you think I'm doing here?"

"Looking for trouble, and not merely some guy you had an argument with."

His smirk vanished. "Yes. In that case, she knows exactly what I'm doing."

Raine frowned. "Come on, Cameron. Let's go."

He sighed as they walked away. Knowing Raine, she would worry about what was going on, and he had hoped to keep any of his trouble away from the students. Not only that, but he still hadn't shaken the feeling of being watched. With a final glance over his shoulder, he headed out of the alley.

CHAPTER THIRTEEN

"Let it go, Raine," Cameron muttered. He frowned at his steak and shook his head. "Even if something is going on, it's not our business. You heard him. The head-mistress knows. This was supposed to be a date night, not a go looking for trouble night."

Raine lifted her glass and swirled the lemonade and ice cubes inside. She resisted the urge to joke about how every night was a looking for trouble night for her. "But maybe we can help him if there's something going on."

"If they need or want our help, they'll ask for it." He shook his head firmly. "Even when you're in the FBI, they'll assign you to specific cases, and there's also jurisdiction to consider. You need to start practicing for that, or will it be you flashing your badge and saying, 'Agent Campbell. Do you know how fast you were going, sir?' Or, 'Do you have a permit for that many chickens?'"

"I won't stop people for speeding as an FBI agent, and do you even need a permit for chickens? You know what?

Never mind." She laughed. "You're not at all curious about what's going on?"

He shook his head. "One thing I trust is my instincts. Whatever was going on there wasn't Professor Powell worried about some man he had an argument with. That was someone ready for a serious fight, and that's not something we should stumble into because of curiosity. I'm a wolf, not a cat, and we all know what happens to curious cats."

She scoffed. "If there's something big going on, that's all the more reason we should look into it."

"No. It's not. I know you want to help people, and like I've said, I'm proud of that. But you're still a student and sometimes, you have to remember that. We all do." He took her hands in his. "Just this one time, you need to back off. If they don't want us involved, it's because it's either not our business, or it's not safe for us. Besides, it's your senior year and you have other things to worry about, like helping Madelyn. You want to be a hero? Be a social hero. Help her learn to be comfortable. The girl's still half-convinced she doesn't deserve to exist. It might not be as exciting to help a shy girl become comfortable in her own skin, but it's equally as important."

Raine sighed and nodded. "You're right. But I smell something going on, and it's like I have to run toward it. I don't like the idea of not doing my part to stop criminals."

Cameron squeezed her hands, let go, and a smile returned. "Don't worry. By the end of next year, your day job will be to help people and deal with scum all the time."

The next evening in the dining hall, Raine twirled some of her pasta around her fork, a smile on her face. Her thoughts focused on something far different than Professor Powell's adventures and conspiracies hidden from the students. Cameron was right. It was time to be a social hero.

"We need to talk about the Halloween Dance."

She looked around the dining room for Madelyn but wasn't surprised to not see her. The girl tended to come first or at the end of the meal hours to minimize her exposure to the other students. As far as she had heard, the elf hadn't been bullied, but the girl had interpreted her early behavior as bullying, so even a well-meaning interaction might be misunderstood.

"What about the dance?" Cameron asked. "You don't like the Power of Nature theme? I thought it was cool. It gives people ideas for some wild stuff but if they only want to come in more normal clothes in a certain color, that works, too. I thought something like the power of the wild forest for me." He rubbed his chin. "There are a lot of possibilities there."

Evie looked at William and her curious look reflected her thoughts. "I thought along the lines of river goddess."

The half-Ifrit chuckled around his bite of salmon and swallowed. "I'll make it easy on myself and go volcano, at least in terms of colors. I like it when themes depend on me accepting my nature."

Raine shook her head. "No."

Cameron, Evie, and William stared at her, disbelief on their faces over her curt dismissal.

She waved her hands in front of her. "I mean, yes, those

are great ideas, but that's not what I was talking about. I'm worried about Madelyn. Last year during Halloween, those spirits almost got her. From what Vianna said, she might even attract them."

Philip nodded. "Sure, but wasn't that not actually about being a Coral Elf but because she was…whatever you want to call her and unstable? She's stable now. That won't happen again. There have been no other times that spirits have messed with her since then."

"Because we didn't have a thinned veil," she pointed out. "And we don't know for certain the spirits will leave her alone simply because she is stable." She shook her head. "The professors probably don't even know that, and Madelyn might not be willing to tell them. I think she understands the World in Between isn't a good place for her, but I don't want her alone when the veil's thin. It's too dangerous. She has good magic, but I could easily see she might panic and not know what to do."

"What's your plan?" Cameron asked. "If you want to try to convince her to go to a dance for fun, I think you should give that up. Even if she wanted to come, it's too big a canyon to jump, and it's the kind of dance where people expect to have a date. She might be ready for friends, but she's not ready for dating."

Adrien cleared his throat. "I have an easy solution. It requires no extra effort from anyone other than me."

They all turned to look at him.

"With Christie gone, I don't have a date." He shrugged. "I planned to volunteer at the dance. Perhaps I can suggest to Madelyn that she also volunteer. It's a way for her to be around people without much in the way of social expectations, and if we're both there, I can keep an eye on her and defend her if anything happens. It helps with several problems at once."

She nodded. "That's a great idea, Adrien. Thank you for suggesting it."

"You still have to get her to agree," the shifter reminded her. "She might simply want to hide in her room at a time when she knows for certain no one will bother her."

"One step at a time. I'll try to talk to her about it."

Raine knocked lightly on Madelyn's door. There was no response and the seconds ticked by before she raised her hand to knock again. The door finally crept open and the Coral Elf peered through the crack, her bottom lip quivering.

She exhaled a sigh of relief and opened the door, stepped aside, and took a deep breath. Her visitor entered and closed the door behind her.

Piles of books covered the desks in the room, which displayed no real decoration or personalization other than the flowered blanket over one bed. The other beds remained unmade. Raine wasn't sure if not giving Madelyn a roommate helped rather than harmed her, but she trusted in Headmistress Berens' judgment and put the thought out of her mind. Just as she had learned to rely on her friends and not try to solve every problem herself, she needed to constantly remind herself to trust in the school staff.

"Hello, Raine," Madelyn said quietly, her voice almost a whisper.

"All these weeks and I've never been in your room." She smiled. "I think you're the only person on campus who likes to read more than I do."

"R-reading is relaxing." The elf took another deep breath. "And I don't have to concentrate on what I'm supposed to say." She sighed. "Is something wrong? Did you not want me to come back to movie night? I know you were all trying to be nice, but you thought my movie was weird."

Although she had attended movie nights since her offering of *Koyaanisqatsi*, her next turn to select a movie hadn't come up. Raine was still absorbing the strange movie, but she wasn't sure she actively disliked it.

She chuckled. "It was definitely weird, but it was also thought-provoking and it helped us understand you a little better, which is a good thing." She shook her head. "And, no, nothing's wrong. I wanted to talk to you about the upcoming Halloween Dance."

Madelyn shook her head frantically. "I d-don't want to go to the dance. There's no one I like anyway, and I'm not good at dancing or choosing costumes. It'd be too much."

"I understand all that, but I also know the best way to learn more about people is to observe them in different social environments." She offered her a soft smile. "Adrien thought of a good way to do that where you don't have to worry about dancing or costumes."

The elf blinked. "What?"

"You can volunteer at the dance. They always need help with the punch and snacks and that kind of thing. Adrien won't dance either, so you can hang out with him doing volunteer things, and that way, you're not alone on Halloween when the rest of the school is having fun."

She looked uncertain. "Won't it be loud?"

"He can help you with sound dampening spells if you aren't good with them already."

Madelyn took three deep breaths and slowly and laboriously released them. She swallowed and looked up. "I-I like the idea. Going to movie night has shown me that normal people won't hate me."

Raine grinned. "I don't know if my friends and I are normal, but I'm glad to hear it."

"I also understand that I have a long way to go. I'm still afraid all the time." The Coral Elf folded her arms across her chest, grabbed her shoulders, and shuddered. "I'm afraid that I'll disappear one day and go back there or someplace like it, or that the PDA will send me there on purpose."

She shook her head. "That won't happen. You have friends and the professors looking out for you now, and we will make sure you get a good start in life."

"I-I keep telling myself that, but it's hard to remember." Madelyn closed her eyes and a small smile formed. "And I know I need to push a little. I'll never be like you, though."

"You don't have to be like me. Just be the girl you want to be. All I want to do is provide you the tools to allow you to pursue that."

The girl opened her eyes and nodded. "Thank you for that, Raine."

CHAPTER FOURTEEN

The mammoth red dragon reared and spread his wings. His roar drowned out all the other sounds. Jagged peaks rose above the beast, but they were irrelevant. The cliff face blocked the Louper team's movement but the small cave opening set in the center of it was the obvious destination.

"I think I prefer all the glass birds we just fought," Dennis mumbled. "Or even those angry bushes from the start of the match."

"Unlike those fights, we'll not win against this thing," Adrien shouted to his team. "We have to try to get past him. We must be close to the token if they have an obstacle like that."

At the start of the match, tracking spells had pointed them in the right direction but they failed immediately before the great glass bird ambush.

The current Cardinals line-up—juniors Hilda and Carlos along with sophomores Dennis and Irina—all strengthened their shields and spread out around Adrien, determination carved into their faces.

The dragon blasted a stream of orange-red flame but thankfully, nowhere near the players. The match designers obviously had some specific trigger in mind.

"Do you think Dallas has a big dragon blocking them on their side?" Dennis asked with a sneer.

"If not a dragon then something equally annoying." The elf shrugged. "And the longer we take trying to decide how to get past this one, the more chance they have to get past theirs."

Irina frowned. "I'll never complain about Dorvu being small or breathing ice ever again."

The captain pointed at the cliff. "It's too tall to burst up, but if we make handholds, we can climb and burst, or simply climb. Maybe a rope and swing up?"

Hilda pointed her wand at the bellowing dragon. "I think he'll have something to say about it. I doubt this is merely a test of bravery."

Dennis grinned. "What you need is a distraction by a brave idiot. If the beast's focused on someone like that, you can all get through."

"That would be handy, yeah. We merely need a few brave idiots." Hilda smirked.

The boy stared at Adrien and saluted. "Volunteering to be an idiot, captain."

The Light Elf snickered, but his smile faded. "If you are eliminated, we'll be a man down. If the Fireflies make it through their obstacle without losing players, it might cost us the match."

"If you have a way through that dragon without bait,

I'm fine with that too, but I honestly doubt the Fireflies could get through something like Angry Red over there without losing at least one player."

Adrien knelt and retrieved a rock. He cast an invisibility spell around it before he hurled it toward the cliff but not directly at the dragon. A few seconds later, the creature breathed a streak of flame that forced the team to duck. The scorched rock reappeared and tumbled to the ground.

"He sensed an invisible rock flying through the air." He shrugged. "The brave idiot plan has grown in appeal."

Dennis layered additional shields on himself and twirled his wand. "Prepare to be impressed."

"We'll let Dennis draw the dragon's attention before we make for the cliff," the captain said. "Go on five, Dennis. One, two, three, four, five."

The boy burst away from the group, a huge grin on his face. He jerked his wand to the side and cast another burst spell to change his direction before the massive beast lumbered toward him with a bone-rattling roar and released his fire. The player's quick shift saved him from incineration and elimination from the match.

He raised his wand and directed an ice lance at his adversary. The spell bounced off the dragon's thick scaly hide but elicited another roar.

Adrien waited a few more seconds before he launched himself upward with a burst spell and the others followed immediately. They approached the cliff, the dragon's back now exposed. The huge creature swung toward them, reared, and ignored another flurry of ice spears from their teammate. Its deadly jet of flame scorched the ground and only barely missed the players.

"We need more idiots," Hilda shouted. "And I doubt we'll have time to create handholds. What about a nested reverse burst?"

The elf frowned. "We've only practiced it a few times, and if you're suggesting what I think, we'll probably only be able to get one player up there."

"We don't have much time to talk about it."

"Fine." He nodded before he burst to the side to disrupt the dragon's tracking. "Hilda, you help Dennis distract the dragon. Carlos and Irina, you help me with the nested burst. I'll get to that cave."

Hilda surged toward the dragon and burst out of the way of another stream of flame while she retaliated with a fireball of her own. Dennis pelted the beast with a volley of summoned snowballs. It backed away, the ground shaking with each step, and roared menacingly.

Adrien, Carlos, and Irina ran toward the cliff. The plan had to work. They might not need an undefeated season prior to the championship, but if they achieved that, it would at least assure them their opportunity.

"Irina, get ready. We need about five more yards," Adrien shouted.

The trio continued their desperate bounced magical advance toward the cliff face as their two teammates did their best mosquito impressions against the mammoth defender. Dennis stumbled on a landing and grimaced as the dragon bathed him in flame.

The elf grabbed Carlos' hand. Irina pointed her wand and shouted her incantation. Both boys soared upward. Adrien let go and rattled off another burst spell to fling himself even higher and the other boy down.

The elf pitched toward the cave opening, but it was clear he didn't have the height to make it. His mastery of the burst spell still required leverage for decent propulsion. It was time for an alternative. He raised his hand and made several quick movements, the incantations fast and easy.

A thin column of rock erupted from the cliff face. He caught it, used it to anchor his swing, and the momentum carried him toward the cave opening. The dragon seared the front of the cliff with fire to toast Irina and Carlos out of the match to join Dennis. Adrien flailed desperately and his fingertips caught the edge of the cave. He hauled himself up, his jaw tight, and expected flames at any moment. Instead, the furious dragon turned his fiery wrath on Hilda.

Adrien was the last Cardinal left but he didn't let his thoughts linger on their losses. His teammates were now spectators, but they still depended on him to make their sacrifices worth it. A quick jog illuminated by a light orb brought him deeper into a maze-like cave. After a few more yards, he cast a tracking spell, surprised that it stabilized.

With the pale white-blue sphere guiding him, he hurried between the walls, a shield spell and sword at the ready. The tracking orb bounced less and less as he moved farther into the maze until abruptly, the darkened rock of the mountain gave way to a vast tree-filled cavern. Glowing fungus lit up the roof like stars at night. Based on his tracking spell, the token was immediately ahead in a pile of leaves that covered a stump in the center of the cave forest.

A smirking elf and a frowning witch crept out of the

trees. The Dallas Fireflies, or what remained of them. He assumed that if more players had survived whatever dragon or obstacle had slowed them, they would have been there in force.

The Light Elf spun and sprinted into the trees to avoid a quick restraint chain from the witch. It was the smart play on the opposing teams' part. They didn't have to eliminate him, only to stall him and search through the pile of leaves to reach the token. A drawn-out battle didn't necessarily play to their strengths, so he launched a few quick fireballs at them. They ducked back among the trees.

He grinned. They had made a critical mistake. Their fireball and light bolt replies struck his tree to explode the bark and kick up a cloud of smoldering wood chunks, but he ignored them and concentrated on a multi-fake spell. Carefully, he forced the magic into three separate streams and focused his mind. It was time to win the match.

Adrien finished the spell and sprinted out of cover, now accompanied by three other versions of himself. One bolted toward the stump and two raced toward the Fireflies, their palms up as if prepared to cast a spell. He ran forward, but not toward the stump.

The Fireflies hesitated for a few seconds before they opened fire again. One directed a chain at the fake running toward the stump and narrowly missed. The other focused on the other two replicas and released a barrage of fireballs that destroyed the nearby trees

Adrien took his chance. He pointed his hand to the side and cast a burst spell to launch himself directly toward his target. The next Dallas attack managed to strike the fake close to him and the image shimmered as a chain passed through it. The opposing players shouted once they realized the real Adrien was almost at the prize.

He thrashed into the pile, knocked the leaves into the air, and provided a small natural cloud of chaff for a few seconds. Ignoring the other players, he jerked his head frantically in his search for the token. The leaves began to settle and both of his opponents launched chains at him.

The elf noticed a small lump under a remaining leaf and brushed it aside to reveal the token. He snatched it up at the same moment that the chains wound around him and secured him. He fell and the impact was hard enough to make him wince. If the blow had knocked the disc free, the other team could argue it was a mere brush and not a true collection.

A few seconds passed as the Dallas players charged forward, huge grins on their faces. He laughed and craned his neck to look at his now open palm. While he might not be able to move, that didn't change the fact that he held the treasure in his hand.

His opponents slowed and disappointment crept onto their faces. They hadn't stopped the Cardinals.

CHAPTER FIFTEEN

Xander slammed his fist on Mara's desk. "I'm frustrated."

The headmistress nodded, her face a mask of calm concern. "I know that, Xander, but maybe it's time to face the fact that your plan might not work. You can keep at it, but I doubt that simply wandering the kemana will draw them out—and that's assuming they're actually there."

"They are there. I know it."

"How?" She frowned. "Has anyone approached you since Syras?"

"No, but I've felt people watching me." He took a deep breath and released it slowly through his nose. "Following me."

"And have you tried to use magic to find them?" Her expression seemed more curious than doubting.

"Yes, but I've not found anyone yet." He pinched the bridge of his nose. "It's like they're toying with me."

"Or you're merely imagining things." Mara shook her head. "You have to face that possibility as well. I'm not saying it's true paranoia. After all, someone did try to kill you. But we have no proof they're in Ruby Falls or anywhere else near this school waiting for you other than a tip from one dubious former dark wizard colleague of yours. The mere fact that you've spent so much time in the kemana will only feed into things more, and for all you know, it might be some other locals who followed you because they're curious about why you spend so much time there."

Xander shook his head. "No. Sometimes, you don't need magic. Sometimes, your instincts can serve you well, and mine tell me there's an assassin in the kemana, waiting for their chance to kill me. I intend to trap him."

"You could restrict yourself to the school grounds," she suggested softly. "How patient could they be? If you don't emerge for months—and this is assuming they are present —they might leave."

"Then I'm living in fear."

"Are you not living in fear now?"

He sighed and slumped in his chair. "I'll have to think about it."

Agent Connor nodded to his trainees where they sat at their table. "I want to thank you both for putting in extra work this semester to catch up because of your summer research trip. I wasn't sure if it would be too much, but we're back on track for what we need, and that's not even counting the practical experience of apprehending those poachers. One thing you've both gained in your time here is exposure to many different field situations, and you both understand the dangers involved." He folded his arms and frowned. "Too many new agents don't always appreciate that. Movies and shows can make the danger seem glamorous."

Raine shook her head. "I'm interested in helping people, not getting in magical duels with criminals."

William uttered a soft snort. "I want to be an agent to help preserve the peace."

"I know you both feel that way, but I think it's a good thing to hear aloud." He gestured to the manila folders in front of them. "We had a good discussion today. I know reviewing some of the different divisions and the like might not seem as interesting as case studies, but it's important to understand the scope of what we do at the FBI." The agent smiled. "I would never have thought I would end up a liaison at a magical school, so you never know where your Bureau career might take you in the future. I think it's especially important for you two since we now have both of you on a fast-track plan."

"About that, Agent Connor." The half-Ifrit sighed.

"What?"

"I know we've discussed when I might join the Bureau, but after thinking about everything and my time here, I've decided one hundred percent that I want to go to college before I join the FBI. I know you've already pulled strings to make opportunities for both Raine and me, and I'm thankful for that, but this is something that has been building in my mind for a while now. I had time to really think about it this summer. I want to make that clear, especially if it means you think this is a waste of your time."

Raine looked from one to the other but didn't say anything. Her future might be a clear path, but she didn't want to try to project that onto her friend and make him uncomfortable.

"You sound very certain this time," Agent Connor said.

"I am." William looked at the folder for a moment before he met the man's gaze. "I'm not saying I'm abandoning the Bureau. I merely want more time to experience what life is like as something other than an FBI agent. I think I'll make a better agent that way. This semester, my friends and I have talked a lot about how much we've changed since coming here, who we are, and what that means. I didn't know who I truly was before I came here." He nodded at Raine. "My friends helped me figure that out, but there are still parts of me out there I need to discover, and so I need more time."

The man nodded slowly. "Most people aren't even allowed to join the agency until they're twenty-three, so you wanting a few more years isn't that strange. I won't say I'm not disappointed that you've chosen to wait, but that doesn't mean your training and studies with me are a waste of time. It simply means you'll be even more prepared when the time comes, and we can still have the age limit waived once you finish college." Something approaching concern entered his face and he looked at Raine. "And you?"

She shook her head. "It might sound arrogant, but I guess I already know who I am. I've known for a long time. I'm supposed to be an FBI agent. The fact that I'm a witch is more or less an extra." She shrugged. "Although it is getting me in early, so I won't complain."

"That's good to hear." Agent Connor turned to stare out a window at some trees swaying in the wind. "It's okay to be uncertain about things. I've changed my mind about magicals in my time here, and that's why I'm so eager to have magicals I trust blazing the trail and changing how our government handles things. In many ways, the FBI, our country, and even the world are still stuck in those years after the gates began opening. Everyone wants to pretend that if they simply close their eyes and wait, things will go back to the way things were. Sure, maybe a neighbor has pointed ears, but America and the world would be the same." His expression turned serious. "I'll be honest. I even thought that way for a while."

Raine blinked. "Really?"

William looked less surprised.

The agent nodded. "I don't think you younger people can ever truly appreciate what it means to grow up in a world where you've been taught your entire life that magic is something you only see in movies—or, at the most, some fringe oddity that might explain a freak miracle here and there. If a witness had come to me and told me how he saw someone disappear, I would have laughed him off or thought he was crazy, but almost overnight, that whole situation changed."

He shook his head. "We found out that magic was real and that humanity wasn't alone. Think about that last part. One of the most important questions of modern times was if humans were the only intelligent species in the universe. Then we found out not only is that not the case, but we're not even the only intelligent species on our planet." He chuckled. "To be honest, when you think about the kind of head-trip from that plus magic being confirmed to be real and common, it's amazing everything didn't fall apart."

The half-Ifrit frowned. "It's not like there wasn't trouble. There still is."

"That's true. There are rogue magicals and magical beasts out of control in some countries. Chaos too. Technology has stagnated slightly and has only now started to move forward again." Agent Connor frowned. "I would prefer if the government didn't have to rely on bounty hunters to do so much heavy lifting with some of the rogue magicals, but there was no grand war of the worlds, nor a local world war. Yes, some individual unstable countries had their problems, but that's how history has always unfolded." He shook his head. "Everything we thought we knew about the world was proven wrong, and humanity's collective response was to shrug and say, 'Okay, that's nice, let's move forward and adapt.' Despite all the dangerous magical criminals and threats out there, you could say it helped restore my faith in my species."

Raine considered that. Her family's involvement in the FBI meant she had no illusions about the horrible things that bad and twisted criminals could do, but somehow, that had never translated into a distrust of humanity as a whole. The way she understood it, if humanity was truly evil at their core, anything approaching civilization would have never arisen.

"And what about your faith in other species?" William asked, his voice low and almost threatening.

Agent Connor shrugged. "The more I learn about different species or races or whatever term you want to use, the more I learn that no matter what they look like or what strange powers they have, they all seem to be motivated by the same kinds of things. Gnomes live for millennia, but most don't appear as strange aliens to me. If I can relate to someone thousands of years old even for a few minutes, I'd argue we have more similarities than differences."

"So you're not afraid of something like the Oriceran Great War?" she asked. "We all have magic now."

He chuckled. "We managed not to nuke ourselves before the gates starting opening. I don't think a few wands will make that much of a difference."

"What about that thing in L.A. a few years back?" William asked with a frown. "When they had to evacuate because some magic nuke or whatever was misplaced?"

"Oricerans and humans cooperated to make sure no one was hurt. To me, it sounds like proof that our planets have a good future. We've kind of gone far off our original subject, but if you want to take anything from what I've said, let me tell you both Earth and Oriceran are worth fighting for. There are bad people on both planets, but there are far more good people." He looked at William. "And we who guard the good people welcome help whether it's later..." He turned to Raine. "Or sooner."

His trainees both smiled.

CHAPTER SIXTEEN

"Do you think we'll run into Professor Powell here?" Raine asked.

Cameron looked around and pointed at some trees with a grin. "I'm sure he's hiding there, waiting for his chance to jump out."

Joking about the sudden appearances of the professor had become common-place since their encounter with him in Ruby Falls. It was a way she dealt with the lingering mystery, and the humor seemed to relax rather than annoy the protective shifter.

She walked with her boyfriend up a wooden path between scattered trees. Some retained leaves, most of them different shades of red and orange, but many had already lost most of their foliage. Green shrubs bordered the walkway but going to a botanical garden on a modestly chilly October day hadn't been her best idea ever, even if the stubbornness of many Virginia flowers added to the color of the surviving fall leaves to make it not entirely pointless. The milder climate of the state had been something she'd grown to appreciate in her time at the School of Necessary Magic.

She zipped her coat after a quick gust of wind. It had been colder that semester, but the real truth was she had gone native. Her Midwest cold tolerance was long gone, and she dreaded the weather when she returned home for the Christmas vacation. The only lengthy amount of time she spent in Michigan anymore was during the summer. Thoughts of weather gave way to the conversation with William and Agent Connor the day before. Doubt, or at least the seed of it, sneaked in.

"You don't think I'm weird, do you?" she asked.

Cameron frowned. "Huh? What are you talking about? For what?" He glanced around and leaned closer. "For being a magical? I thought we were talking about Professor Powell."

"Forget him. You don't think I'm weird because I'm so set on going to the FBI?" Raine shrugged. "I never thought so, but every once in a while, someone says something or something happens, and I ask myself if I'm doing the right thing. When Agent Connor told me I could go to the academy right after graduation, I was ecstatic. I always saw college as another distraction from my real goal."

"It's not weird." He shook his head firmly. "It's called planning and dedication. I admire it. I know I've been an idiot sometimes because I've worried about what it meant for me, and if that's why you think you're weird, get that out of your head right now. You should be concerned about finishing school and going into the academy, not about me. We'll find a way that works for you and me."

"That's not it. I mean, I do care and think about you, but

in this case, it's more what happened with William. It didn't bother me at the time, but I wondered if I was weird being so set on what I would do. It's not like he's turning his back on the FBI. He simply wants more time to prepare and live life, and I'm like, 'If they would let me join the FBI tomorrow, I would go.'"

"If we're being honest, you're not weird. The only weird one in the Trouble Squad is me by a long shot." Cameron snorted. "Don't ever let Philip know I admitted that."

"What do you mean?" She leaned closer. "How are you weird? You can't be upset about being a shifter, right? Even non-magicals don't care that much anymore. If anything, they might care less than many wizards. They had that shifter run for Congress and almost win, and I wouldn't be surprised if in a few years, we have a shifter representative. Maybe he'll even be a School of Necessary Magic graduate."

"Maybe, but I don't want to run for Congress." He frowned. "And this has nothing to do with me being a shifter."

"What then?" She looked at her boyfriend with concern. He was always so obsessed with protecting her, but she wanted to do what she could to protect his heart.

"It's like this. You'll go into the FBI. So will William. Adrien will be a Guardian—and by the way, think about how he's basically known that since he was a little elf you could probably stick on a shelf, so it makes your FBI obsession look mild by comparison. Sara will be an artist. Evie will become an apprentice potions witch. Philip will go to college and then either work for a charity or an NGO. The only person who doesn't know what he'll do with his future is me. I'm the weirdo, not you because I don't have a clue at all about what I'm supposed to do with my life. I keep having ideas, but the minute I think about them too long, they don't seem like good ones anymore."

"So what?" Raine squeezed his hand gently. "Many people don't have their entire future mapped out in their senior year of high school. I don't think it's a big deal. If everyone in the world knew what they wanted to do with the rest of their life that early, it would be a very different planet. Same thing for Oriceran."

Cameron watched an older couple walk a parallel path in the distance. "I've studied military history for a while now. For a long time, I thought I might want to join the military, especially since they've talked about wanting to recruit magicals to special units. I thought as a shifter serving the country, I could do my part to show that we're good and patriotic to non-magicals. Despite what you said, dark wizard propaganda has done a lot to poison both magicals and non-magicals against my kind, but now..." He shook his head. "It'll sound stupid."

She touched his arm to encourage him. "But what? You can tell me. Nothing you might say will ever sound stupid to me. You have to know that by now, Cameron."

"If I join the military, who knows where they might send me? Especially nowadays. I could end up in a desert or jungle hunting magical monsters for two years and barely able to talk to you. I have a lot of respect for the guys who can do that, but whatever I choose for the future, I want it to include you and sooner rather than later. We might not live right next to each other at first, but I don't want to take a job that will guarantee I'll be sent far away.

Maybe that's selfish, but it's how I feel. Even my pack understands that."

"You're thinking about this way too hard." Raine crouched to inhale the earthy scent of a patch of chrysanthemums. More and more color had filtered onto the sides of their walking path. They must have reached a denser patch of late-blooming flowers. "Sometimes, it merely takes a while. Remember that."

"Meaning what? What takes a while?"

"If you're not sure what you want to do, go to college and study things that will be useful no matter what you do." She tried to keep her tone light. "For at least the first couple of years, that will be easy enough. By then, we'll both have a better understanding of where we both need to be, and you can make decisions from there. It works for millions of other teens. I don't see why it wouldn't work for you."

Cameron remained standing but smiled at the flowers. "A little bit more history and psychology wouldn't hurt. As a start, that is. I find them interesting, too."

"Exactly. I'm not saying stall. I'm only saying take your time to think about what you really want to do." Raine straightened, a warm smile on her face. "You know what I think?"

"What?"

"You're a protector at heart. I know you'll end up doing a job involving that. Maybe it won't be the FBI or the military, but they aren't the only people out there who defend people who can't defend themselves. I think the best way to be happy in a job is to go into one that takes advantage of your instincts. I itch to solve mysteries and help people, so even without my dad, I would have been a natural fit for the FBI. You merely need to find a job that makes the most advantage of your instincts."

"A protector, huh? I suppose there are many paths out there to getting a job protecting people. I know my pack would like me close to them, but like I said, they also understand that I need to be part of the world and part of your life. A pack can support its members even if they're spread out." He pointed to dark clouds on the horizon. "But speaking of protection, I think right now, we need to get going so I can protect you from the rain."

She laughed. "I should have suggested this earlier in the semester."

"Probably." He grinned. "You always make me feel better about myself, Raine. I don't say that enough, but I want you to know it."

Her cheeks heated. "Same here. You've made it easier for me to face all the troubles I have in my time here."

"Good." He leaned in and kissed her on the forehead. "I love you."

"I love you, too."

CHAPTER SEVENTEEN

A few days later, Raine stepped into the library and swept the room with a careful gaze. She wasn't there for books or even enlightening conversation with Head Librarian Decker. After a short search, she located her target, a blue-haired girl with a flowered backpack, and made her way over to her.

"Hey, Madelyn," she said with a smile.

The sophomore looked up from her current book, *Philosophical Dualism in Light of the Revelations of Magic: The Oxford Symposium Review.* "Hello."

Raine glanced at the book. Her mind was focused on more practical mysteries. She could help the girl by being a friend, not by soothing her philosophical concerns. "I had a question for you, especially since we only have a week before the dance."

"O-okay, what?" She blinked her red eye and green eye and the heterochromia only made her look more confused for some reason.

"Most of us have decided we won't go in costume but will rather use special colors to communicate our themes. Everyone else has their stuff, but I still need to go to the kemana and find some color- and pattern-changing fabric. Would you like to come with me? I guess that's one question, but I also wanted to know if you were allowed to go into the kemana? I've been meaning to ask you for a while, but I haven't had a good reason to."

Madelyn nodded. "Headmistress Berens says Ruby Falls is fine, but I shouldn't go into Charlottesville. I haven't gone because it's too stressful by myself. A-and I'm not dressing up special for the dance since I'm only volunteering."

"Sure, I know, but I thought it might be fun for us. Since it's only me rather than the whole big group, it'd be less stressful. Two friends hanging out, you know?" She summoned her brightest smile.

The elf took a deep breath and gave a shallow nod. "Okay. I'll do it."

"Great." Raine clapped once and grimaced when Joe shook a finger at her from the front desk and the flower on his bowler hat growled. "See you on Saturday, Madelyn."

The Coral Elf clutched her friend's hand as they walked down the street. She winced every time anyone came around the corner as if they would be attacked at any moment even though no one paid her much attention.

Raine's fabric rested in the bag she held in her other

hand. She would still need to call in a few favors to have it made into a proper dress. Having magic wasn't a substitute for actual design skills, but she had enough time to talk to the appropriate people.

"This isn't so bad, right?" she asked. "And Hap was fun, wasn't he?"

"I liked his hat." Madelyn sighed. "S-sorry. It's only that before, it was easy because I always hid behind Vianna. I know I shouldn't fear these people any more than I do the people at the school, but what my rational mind tells me is different than what I feel."

Cina stood in the distance and chatted with an Arpak woman. The witch looked at Raine and Madelyn and blinked a few times in what looked like surprise before she turned and left, almost in a run. The Arpak woman stared after her and muttered something, but Raine couldn't make it out. She wondered if she should get involved, but Cameron's words about being a social hero kept her focused. Even someone as nice as Cina would have arguments with people, and she didn't need a busybody young witch to interfere in them—at least when said busybody young witch was already busy with something else.

She directed them around a corner. "I'm not sure if you will like Bubble & Fizz. We used to go there when we first started at the school, but lately, it's died off for us. But you're a little younger—but not younger at the same time, I suppose." She shook her head. "That probably doesn't make much sense. I mean you're into things like classical Russian literature and philosophy. You make me feel like a slacker."

"S-sorry." Madelyn sighed.

She laughed. "There's nothing to be sorry about. I'm only saying you don't have the concerns many of the other sophomores, let alone people your actual age, have. It's hard to decide what you might like."

A pale light-haired young man with a broad smile hurried after them from across the street. The smile combined with the jeans and *Always See the Bright Side* T-Shirt gave him a casual vibe, but something about it felt fake.

Raine glanced at him as they headed farther up the street. She didn't recognize him, and he continued to smile at her but didn't immediately close the distance.

Her stomach knotted and her FBI trainee instincts screamed a warning. She tightened her grasp on Madelyn's hand. "Hey, maybe I should show you Bubble & Fizz after all." She picked up the pace, led her friend up the street, and made several quick turns, but when she looked back, the man remained stubbornly behind them.

"One second, Madelyn," She stopped, set her bag down, and raised her hand to her jacket and the wand inside.

The Coral Elf turned and blinked in confusion. "What's wrong?"

"Nothing yet, and hopefully, nothing will be." She narrowed her eyes and waited while the man sauntered up to them, his hands in his pockets. If he had a wand, it was well-hidden, but he could be a race that didn't need one for magic.

"Can I help you?" Raine asked, her tone polite. She had stopped on a street with a few different vendors and two shops with open windows. Witnesses helped to keep things under control and might provide reinforcements.

He smiled. "You go to the School of Necessary Magic, right?"

Madelyn grabbed her arm and stepped behind her, shaking.

Raine narrowed her eyes. "Yes, we do. What about it?"

"Professor Xander Powell teaches there, doesn't he?" The man's smile didn't reach his eyes. Something about them felt cold and almost dead.

"Yes." She gripped the shaft of her wand. Her heart pounded and Madelyn continued to tremble behind her.

"Don't worry, little witch." He tilted his head and there seemed to be something almost unnatural about the movement. "I don't mean you any harm. I only need you to deliver a message to my old friend, Xander." He held his hand up to reveal a solid black ring carved with Futhark runes. "It's a very simple message. You won't even have to write it down."

Raine backed away, her other arm up and in front of Madelyn. "And you can't simply get it to him yourself?"

"I have my reasons for avoiding that, which are best for everyone involved." The man chuckled quietly. "Tell him to come to the Crystal Fields Inn on November 1st at noon. If he doesn't, it'll be like Marseilles."

"And what happened there?"

"Don't worry about it, little witch. It's not your affair." He half-turned and regarded her with the cold, empty expression. "Just deliver the message."

A few wizards stepped out of a shop, their wands in their hands, and watched the light-haired man with suspicion as he walked down the street.

"W-who was that?" Madelyn asked.

"I have absolutely no idea." Raine shook her head. "See, this is what I was talking about to Cameron."

"What?"

"I try to stay out of trouble, and somehow, it finds me." She threw up her hands in disgust.

CHAPTER EIGHTEEN

Xander frowned as Raine stepped out of Mara's office. The girl had delivered her report on what had happened, her FBI pre-training obvious in her attention to detail. She had immediately returned to the school, found the headmistress, and explained the situation. Mara had, in turn, called Bruce and Xander so they could hear her explanation.

The FBI agent now stood near the desk with a tight frown. Mara merely looked exhausted.

"I was concerned about this," she said. "We can't risk the students. I thought this wasn't a problem after the incident with Eris, but I was obviously mistaken."

The wizard shook his head. "Whoever this was didn't attack them, and I don't think he plans to, but I do think this was meant to encourage me to heed his message." He scoffed. "Which was unnecessary since I was looking for him anyway, but message received. I'm more than happy to meet with my secret admirer."

She sighed. "But this would involve going to a place they selected on the designated day. It's obviously a trap."

"I have a target now and a location and an exact time. I've wandered the kemana trying to make enough noise to garner attention, and it's finally worked. There's no way I can pass up the chance to end it." He snorted impatiently and his hands twitched in anticipation.

"November 1st," Bruce murmured. "That isn't much time. And what happened in Marseilles?"

Xander took a deep breath and released it slowly. "I wasn't involved in it and I don't want to talk about it, other than to note there was a cover-up at the kemana and innocent people died. They claimed it was an accident. It wasn't."

"I see. And is there anything special about the Crystal Fields Inn?"

"I've eaten there before. It's nothing special." He frowned and looked a little thoughtful. "It's simply another inn in Ruby Falls. The food isn't even that good. It's like they're afraid to season anything decently. And if you want to ask if I ate there before I was poisoned, I honestly don't remember, but there's a good chance of it."

Mara sighed. "And who is this man? I didn't want to subject Raine or especially Madelyn to something like opposite-eye or similar magic, but perhaps it's necessary."

Xander shook his head. "That won't help."

"You don't think knowing exactly what he looks like would help?"

"No," he replied. "Especially because of the ring."

Bruce lowered his arms and nodded. "The ring? What about it?"

"Raine's description left me no doubts. I used to know a wizard in my bad old days who wore a ring like that. Alfonso, but he was olive-skinned and dark-haired. He looked older, like me, and actually took a lot of pride in not modifying his appearance much. I knew him a long time ago, even before the other friends of mine who were killed." He shrugged.

"It sounds like we have a suspect then," the agent said. "This Alfonso must be the one who wants you dead."

"He didn't have a connection to the other wizards."

The man raised an eyebrow. "You didn't run in any of the same circles at all? Maybe he established a relationship with them after you moved on."

Mara looked at Xander expectantly.

He chuckled. "It's not that, it's more that I've never been much of a necromancer."

"Excuse me?" Bruce frowned.

"I knew Alfonso when I was very young. You could say he was a mentor of sorts." He shrugged. "He was killed—assassinated before I got heavily involved in dark magic."

"You're sure? It's not like wizards don't have their ways to fake things."

"I saw it with my own eyes. I was there when he was killed." He scoffed. "He could have faked it, but I don't understand why he would and more than that, why he would fake his own death and then wait decades to contact me again. If it's about having the skill to eliminate me like Mara suggested a while back, he had it already."

"And who killed Alfonso?" Mara asked

"That I don't know. I was never sure who killed him. I tried to look into it but I lacked the contacts and knowledge I have now, and many people weren't surprised that a wizard who dabbled so much in dark magic would end up dead. He had some...unorthodox ideas that many dark wizard families didn't appreciate either. But the same applies. The kind of people who could kill Alfonso aren't the kind of people who would need to train to do the same to me."

"What do you mean, he had unorthodox ideas?" the agent asked. He moved to the empty chair in front of Mara's desk and sat.

"He cared far less about dark wizards controlling things then many of the families," Xander said. "He argued that their failure to establish and maintain control proved they weren't worthy, so he wasn't supportive of many dark wizard plans."

Bruce nodded. "And who did he think should be running things?"

Xander shrugged. "He was never really clear on that. His main obsession was with how open struggle made people stronger. He wasn't much for schemes. I often wondered if that's what got him killed. Although he wouldn't purposefully assassinate another dark wizard, I could see how him annoying them might have led to some thinking he was better off dead."

Mara sighed. "Why didn't you mention him earlier when all this came up?"

"How is a dead man important? I had no reason to suspect he was involved, even indirectly."

"He's important because whoever killed him has probably now targeted you," the agent pointed out. "Or if not them, their associates. If he was killed because he defied the dark wizard order, it only stands to reason someone might try to completely remove his influence from the world."

"But like I said, why wait? They could have done it when I was not as skilled as some of the upperclassmen at this school." He looked down and remembered Alfonso's stern gaze and lessons. Sometimes, he'd thought the man was incapable of smiling, but that was another life. A different century. "That's a long time to clean up a mess."

"Perhaps because you didn't immediately follow in his footsteps ideologically." Bruce gestured to Mara. "And it cost you." She averted her gaze.

Xander's jaw tightened. "You're saying they decided I was exactly what they needed, so they let me live?"

The other man nodded. "I know you don't like to talk about that time in your life, but it's obviously related to this. Can you honestly say you were doing anything to disrupt the general plans of the kind of people who might have had a problem with Alfonso? Even if you weren't an enthusiastic supporter, it didn't matter as long as you didn't actively interfere with their plans. You've said it yourself. Dark wizards are about setting up a new world order, not ruthlessly slaughtering people like animals."

"So what? They decided my coming back and helping at this school makes me a threat to their plans?"

"Maybe." Bruce's gaze cut from Mara to Xander. "But they had no reason to really question you until the big battle. That was the point when you proved beyond anything that you weren't loyal to their cause." He pointed at the headmistress. "You proved you were loyal to hers."

She gave a shallow nod. "It makes sense when you think

about it. You helped disrupt major dark wizard plans. We don't even know exactly when the poisoning happened. It could have been shortly after the battle and it took time for the symptoms to fully manifest."

"I doubt it with the timing of the other deaths, but maybe. Alfonso was right to hate all this scheme garbage." Xander scowled in irritation. "So you think dark wizards have finally come to finish the job?"

"Much of the evidence points that way," Bruce confirmed.

"We've strengthened the school's defenses too much," Mara added. "It's all but impossible for them to strike us directly. And the additional efforts after the Eris incident might have effectively made it impossible. That would explain their desperation."

"You're saying the timing with the other killings is a coincidence?" He raised an eyebrow.

"I don't know, but the evidence constantly points back to your past with dark magic." She sighed. "I don't know what else to think."

The agent tapped his foot on the floor, his expression thoughtful. "Evidence leads the case, but instincts lead to evidence. Either it's these people, or someone's gone to a lot of trouble to make it seem that way. The question now is how we want to handle this. We could contact the PDA —maybe Oliver. I'm sure she could get some additional help."

Xander snorted. "I'm tired of everyone else cleaning up my mistakes."

"Please," Mara said, her voice plaintive. "If these people

are assassins and killers, they're criminals and law enforcement should be involved."

"We don't know what's going on. All we know is someone went to a lot of trouble to poison me and slowly kill a few other dark wizards, and they might be connected to the people who killed Alfonso. I'll accept their invitation. It's away from the school. The way I see, even in the worst-case scenario, that keeps the students safe. We won't repeat what happened before."

Bruce frowned and shook his head. "In the worst-case scenario, you might end up dead."

The wizard grinned. "Don't worry. I have a few days to put my affairs in order."

"That's not funny, Xander," Mara protested.

"Then let's simply say the other guy has a few days to put his affairs in order."

CHAPTER NINETEEN

R aine shifted on the couch to get comfortable next to Cameron. She glanced at Madelyn as Sara stepped in with the night's DVD. The Coral Elf had been extra nervous following the encounter in the kemana, but her eager smile for movie night proved that a little extra friendship could do a lot to soothe a nervous soul. While she hadn't wildly changed since the beginning of the semester, she seemed more comfortable around the Trouble Squad and even ate with them on occasion. By the end of the year, Raine wanted to help Madelyn find a regular group of friends in her own grade. It wouldn't help if she slipped back into her old self once the others graduated.

"I wanted to switch things up," the kitsune announced with a smile, still near the television. "And I got the idea of something a little lighter with DiCaprio after Cameron's *Gangs of New York* selection the last time."

Cameron grunted. "I liked it."

"It was okay, but it's definitely not in the top tier of DiCaprio movies."

Evie made a face. She had been very vocal on the last movie night about not enjoying the choice, even if the shifter justified it as "having historical basis despite creative liberties." That was her main problem. It was easier for her to dismiss purely fictional violence, but anything based on actual events, even if fancifully elaborated, tended to disturb her.

Raine had worried Madelyn would be rattled by the movie as well, but she admitted she found it fascinating to watch a historically-based movie even if she had trouble wrapping her mind around vengeance as a motivation. Whether that was a reflection of her odd view of the world or merely evidence of a kind soul remained unclear. Every film they watched with the girl gave the group that much more insight into her fundamental personality.

Sara opened the DVD case as the Coral Elf settled in on another couch. She sat with a bowl of popcorn and a small bag of peanut butter M&M's in her lap. While she didn't have much of a sweet tooth, she did really enjoy M&M's. Oddly enough, she demonstrated an almost visceral disgust of other candy, and Raine wondered if that implied anything about her biology. The girl remained a mystery in many ways, one that tickled her instincts, even though she understood she wouldn't be the one who could solve all of them.

"Something lighter?" Raine asked. "And it has DiCaprio?" She ran through the possibilities. The actor had some particular comedic gems in the 2030s when he had been dubbed the "Second-Coming of Leslie Nielsen" but had since retreated into serious roles and constantly implied he intended to retire, even though he kept making films. There were also a few decent lighter movies from before that period, but she would need more clues to figure it out.

Sara nodded, an eager smile on her face. "Not only is it lighter than *Gangs of New York*, but it also has romance."

Raine tensed. She didn't like where this was going.

Cameron looked at her with concern. "What's wrong?"

"Lighter?" she repeated. "With romance? Define lighter for me."

The kitsune shrugged. "Well, it's less violent, I guess. Uh, technically more people die in it, but it's not from all the street fights and stabbings and that kind of thing. There are some shootings. I'll admit that. Some beatings, too, but definitely not as bad as the other movie."

"Oh no." She face-palmed. "You're kidding me. You picked that film as your lighter choice?"

Sara offered a sheepish grin. "Yes?"

Adrien frowned from his chair. "What is it? What movie are you talking about?"

"*Titanic.*" Raine shook her head. "That's your idea of a lighter DiCaprio movie, Sara? What about any of his more recent comedies? What about *The Dragon Sitter* or even *Help, My Troll's Got Anger Management Issues?* Heck, even *A Wand, A Will, and a Way?* That one has funny parts but still has serious stuff about Earth and Oriceran interactions."

The other girl scoffed and rolled her eyes. "*Titanic*'s a classic. No one will even remember those other films in ten years, but I did laugh at the troll movie. Anyway, I feel *Titanic*'s a great balance." She smiled. "It has romance for those of us who like romance, and it has a disaster for those who want a little more action." She slipped the DVD in. "Something for everyone. That's why it made so much money."

Madelyn leaned forward, a curious look on her face. "I've been meaning to see this. I read a book about the disaster, and this movie came up in a discussion of media depictions of the event."

Philip sighed and stood. He marched to the door.

"Where are you going?" Sara asked. "Is this some sort of protest?"

"No. I merely think we'll need boxes of tissues." He shrugged.

"Oh. Good call."

The lilting sounds of the flute melody of "My Heart Will Go On" played as the menu came up. Raine took a deep breath. Maybe they should schedule a *Notebook/Titanic* double-feature night, all the concentrated depressing classic romance they could handle.

Madelyn's face was a mess of tears and snot as the final credits rolled. Sara gave her an apologetic look and a few of her own tears escaped. Evie was crying too, but not nearly as badly as the Coral Elf. Adrien stared at the television, deep in thought with his eyes narrowed, and muttered under his breath. William constantly glanced around the room and obviously tried to keep himself from tearing up.

"Jack did the right thing," Cameron declared as Sara

ejected the disk. "He didn't have any magic or anything, so he did the only thing he could. He was a real man to go down protecting his woman like that."

The elf tried to say something, but she managed only a gurgle. She grabbed another tissue from the box beside her and dabbed at her tears. Three other empty boxes littered the couch.

Raine was too worried about Madelyn to be emotionally affected by the movie, even though it normally bothered her. It was hard to predict what might affect the girl. She had demonstrated an almost clinical detachment to *Gangs of New York* despite the higher levels of depicted brutality, but the night's current film had destroyed her.

"No, Jack didn't do the right thing." Adrien leaned back in his chair. "Jack was a fool." He folded his arms. "He threw his life away for nothing. Like I said, a fool."

Everyone stared at him. Madelyn, Evie, Cameron, and Sara all glared. Philip looked confused. Raine merely sighed.

Cameron growled. "Are you serious? You think he didn't do the right thing? What should he have done? Alternated with Rose? She would have ended up with hypothermia too, and they would both be dead. Would you have made Christie alternate?"

"We both have magic, and we wouldn't have been on an ancient boat." The Light Elf shook his head. "Setting that aside, if they both positioned themselves properly, there would have been enough space on the wood so no one had to be in the water." He pointed at the television. "So, he threw his life away for nothing. Yes, Rose went on to a happy and fulfilled life, but don't you think she would have been happier with Jack still alive?"

The shifter uttered another growl but didn't say anything and instead, averted his eyes.

Sara folded her arms, a triumphant and contemptuous smile on her face. "I've heard people say that before, but it's like they forget they just got done watching a movie about a boat sinking and everything involved in that."

"Meaning what?" Adrien asked with a frown.

She simulated waves with her hand. "It wasn't magic wood. Exactly like the lifeboats weren't magic. If a lifeboat could take everyone, they would have listened to Molly Brown and piled people onto them, but they couldn't because there was no space. It's also about buoyancy, and that water was cold enough to kill. Everyone understood that, especially Jack."

Philip nodded his agreement, but whether it was because he believed Sara's argument or simply didn't want to anger his girlfriend wasn't clear.

"You're saying that if they both got on the panel, it would have gone under?" Adrien didn't look convinced.

Madelyn had regained control and only an occasional sniffle escaped. Her face and eyes remained red, but she watched Sara and Adrien with more curiosity than sadness.

"Exactly." The kitsune snapped her fingers. "Then, it would have been a true tragedy. You've never gone swimming in a pool and had two people try to get on a floaty, and it sinks?"

He shook his head. "I can't say that I have, but I'll admit

your explanation does make some sense. I'll have to reconsider my position."

Sara glanced at Madelyn. "What do you think?"

Raine grimaced. The girl had barely stopped crying and they wanted her to focus on the saddest scene in the movie.

The Coral Elf took a deep breath and let it out slowly. She nibbled on her lip before she nodded. "I agree with you. I don't think it was buoyant enough. They would have ended up exposed to the water too much, and both would have died." She sighed. "It's strange."

Raine smiled. Sara had reflexively included her in the conversation without worrying too much. It was a good instinct.

The kitsune looked confused. "Strange?"

"Movies. Stories. The people aren't real in this movie. I know some of them are based on real people, but Jack and Rose aren't." Madelyn grabbed another tissue and dabbed at her glistening eyes. "But I feel their pain like it's real."

"That's what a good movie does." The other girl shrugged. "I know you told us before you like movies that don't have a lot of story and dialog and stuff, but it seems like you're enjoying normal movies a lot, too."

"Enjoyment? Is that what this is?" She looked curious. "But it hurts."

"We all want to feel different emotions. That's what it means to be alive." Raine smiled at Cameron, who wasn't brooding as much since Sara had defended Jack's honor. "And I think experiencing a range of emotions helps us better understand others."

"Contrast," the Coral Elf murmured. "You can't know what true happiness is unless you've experienced sadness.

Happiness without contrast is nothing more than satisfaction masquerading as something more."

"Not exactly how I would have put it, but yes, basically." Raine shrugged. "That's why we watch all kinds of movies together, whether they are sad, funny, scary, or thought-provoking. A good movie makes you feel something. But not every single one can make everyone feel something, which is why we go through different movies and genres."

Madelyn glanced at the television. "I definitely felt something, but next time, can we watch a happy movie?"

She smiled. "Sure. I think it's your pick."

The girl sighed with relief. "Then I'll definitely choose a happy movie."

CHAPTER TWENTY

The heat from the dancing suffused the room and everyone enjoyed the Halloween Dance. Raine swayed with Cameron as soft music played. Her blue-and-white dress shimmered. Lines of white traversed the front and back—her attempt at a dress representing water, both rain and the flow of rivers. Cameron's suit was a mix of greens, browns, and blacks, which shifted with the lighting. He'd demonstrated how it was effective forest camouflage, but not many people at the dance understood what he had intended. She hadn't either at first, but he didn't seem to care all that much about his thematic failure.

"This will be our last Halloween Dance at this school," she murmured. "It's special in a way."

He smiled. "We'll have many other dances in the future, and we've had plenty here. All dances with you are special."

"I'm only saying it makes you think." She glanced at a corner table. Adrien, Madelyn, and a few others had volunteered to help with the refreshments—punch and cookies mostly—but she didn't see her friends anywhere. "I expected to be sadder tonight—sadder at every event that reminded me of the passing of senior year—but the more weeks that go by, the more excited I get about joining the FBI."

"That's a good thing." Cameron repositioned his hand on her waist. "It's always better to look forward to something, right?" He shrugged. "It's simply you being you and then you'll have a whole new challenge."

"Yes, I suppose I will. I'm not worried about the academy, but I do know it'll be a big adjustment after being here for four years." Raine lowered her head to his shoulder but jerked it up when she saw Adrien wave to her from the side of the room with both hands. "What's going on?"

The shifter looked at their friend. "I don't know. He's definitely trying to get our attention and not simply anyone's." He dropped his arms. "I'm sure he has a good reason."

Her heart rate kicked up as they hurried over to the elf.

He frowned before he glared at some of the other volunteers. "I stepped out only for a second to go to the bathroom, and when I came back, Madelyn was gone. No one else even knows where she went. These people have the observation skills of bricks." His hands curled into fists. "I even asked them to keep an eye on her."

"Should we tell a professor?" Cameron asked.

"We don't want to get her in trouble or stress her out if she thinks she's in trouble."

"What if she's seeking out something from the World in Between again?"

Raine shook her head. "I don't think she would. She doesn't need them as friends anymore now that she has us." She took a deep breath. "Let's look around ourselves. If we can't find her quickly, we'll find a professor."

The boys nodded and both headed toward a hallway leading to an exit. Raine was glad her dress had a high hemline. If she had to run around outdoors, it would help. She kicked her heels off as they entered the hallway.

Cool evening air caressed her face as the trio stepped outside and searched for any sign of Madelyn without success.

"Tracking spell?" she suggested.

"Maybe." Adrien frowned.

A scream cut through the night. It sounded feminine but not like Madelyn. Raine immediately sprinted toward the sound and her bare feet squished in the moist grass and dirt. She wanted to believe her friend wouldn't make the same mistake as last year but she couldn't take the risk.

Cameron barreled after her and his eyes flashed yellow. "Be careful. You don't even have your wand."

"I can still punch them."

"What if it's a spirit?"

"I can say mean things. That's much the same thing."

"That's nothing like punching." He sighed.

Adrien summoned a sword as he raced alongside his friends. Another scream followed and the air thickened around them. Raine's stomach lurched, and the world spun for a moment. She shook her head and continued toward a bright flash of light ahead.

Raine turned the corner. A freshman witch stood pressed against the wall, her eyes wide. Her dress cycled through shades of red and orange. Madelyn stood in front of the girl, her palm out and her face pinched in concentration. Her eyes were half-closed. A humanoid spectral form with glowing blue eyes hovered a few yards away from them with an outstretched arm.

The shifter growled. "This is bad."

Adrien released the energy fueling his sword and raised his hand. "Maybe a few focused bolts of magical energy will scare it off."

"No!" Madelyn shouted. Her breathing turned ragged. "I'm restraining it, but it's taking all my concentration. If you do something, you might cause it to break free. Save the other girl first."

Raine crooked a finger at the witch. "Come on. You need to get away."

The girl nodded with a squeak, took a few careful steps past the elf and away from the spirit, and broke into a sprint.

"Go with her to make sure she's safe, Adrien," Raine said. He nodded and rushed after her.

Cameron stared at the spirit. "That's some impressive magic, Madelyn."

"I'm actually not sure how I'm doing it. It's not like the Coral Elf magic that comes naturally or the spells I've learnt from the professors." Madelyn gritted her teeth. "It's like instinct. Vianna and I went through that tear so many times, it's as if holes in the world close by resonate with me."

"Find a professor, Cameron," Raine said. "I'll stay with Madelyn."

"And do what without your wand?" He frowned.

"Talk to her." Raine gave him her best stubborn face. Reluctantly, he sighed and raced away.

The spirit hadn't moved forward. Its form floated and shimmered in the dim night and remained as silent as death.

"That's a useful skill," Raine said. "I'm a senior, and even after all those classes with Professor Powell, I still can't pull something like that off."

Madelyn uttered a harsh laugh. "It's merely proof that I'm strange."

"Strange? We're all strange here. I thought you understood that by now. It's a magic school. I grew up not even knowing I had magic, but I didn't worry that much about going back to my old life. Earth and Oriceran are intertwined now, and it's hard to say what or who is weird or normal. Maybe in the future, everyone will be a magical."

The elf swayed slightly. "I'm so tired. It's taking all my strength to keep it in place."

"We could make a run for it," she suggested. "I'll be with you. I won't leave you behind, no matter what. I don't care that I don't have my wand."

"I feel like if I stop what I'm doing, I'll fall. I can't run." She drew a few deep breaths and sweat trickled down her face. "All these protections and these kinds of things still get through."

"They do warn everyone to not wander on Halloween." Raine stared at the spirit and for any sign of forward movement, but despite its gentle vertical bounce, it was otherwise immobile. "Speaking of which, why did you leave the dance? You could have gone back to your room without going outside."

Madelyn smiled. "Because I was curious. I wasn't looking for one of these if that's what you're thinking, not that I haven't given you a reason to think that after what I did last year."

"You were curious?" Raine asked. "About what? The veil thinning?"

She shook her head. "I was curious if someone would be as stupid as I was. Then I saw the girl and...I had to do something. Instinct kicked in, and for some reason, I wasn't scared."

"You had to help someone in need. I know the feeling." She turned at the sound of movement behind her. Professor Hudson rushed toward them, her wand in hand. Cameron and Adrien accompanied her, but the freshman witch was nowhere in sight. "It looks like reinforcements are here."

Professor Hudson slowed and raised her wand. She whispered an incantation and made several precise movements before she pointed her wand at the spirit. It faded over several seconds until it vanished completely.

Madelyn sighed and collapsed to her hands and knees. "That was hard."

The professor looked at the girl with concern. "Are you all right?"

"I'm only tired."

Raine walked over to Madelyn and extended her hand. "You can lean on me."

The girl stood slowly, her knees shaking. "I-I was scared, but I didn't let that stop me."

She draped the elf's arm over her shoulder and slid hers around her waist to support her. "It's not like I'm not scared when I face something dangerous. I'm proud of you, Madelyn. This proves you're stronger than you thought. You saved that girl from being taken to the World in Between."

Madelyn shook her head as they started walking. "It's because you and the others have helped me."

"All we did was pull out the girl who was already in there."

A silent Cameron and Adrien took positions on either side of them like bodyguards.

Professor Hudson cleared her throat and pointed her wand back in the direction of the building. "Perhaps we should go where students don't have to face dangerous beings from the other side."

Madelyn looked at the witch, slight fear on her face. "Will I be in trouble?"

The woman shook her head. "You saved a fellow student. That's not the kind of thing we tend to punish around here. Obviously, given the situation, you didn't have time to find a professor, but fortunately, your friends did. I also think you made a new friend in the girl you saved."

Madelyn's weary smile still lit up her face. "A new friend?"

Professor Hudson nodded. "Saving someone's life can have that effect, but let's get you where you can rest."

"Sure, rest sounds good." Her eyes closed and she slumped forward.

Cameron stepped forward and scooped the lithe girl into his arms. "This might work out better."

"Thanks," Raine said.

The professor clucked her tongue. "Recruiting the next generation for your FBI Trouble Squad?"

Raine laughed. "Something like that."

CHAPTER TWENTY-ONE

Xander and Mara stepped into the common room of the Crystal Fields Inn. There was nothing unusual about the room itself—no strange concentrations of magic and nothing notable about the wooden tables and chairs or the light orbs used as illumination. There was, however, a conspicuous lack of other patrons or staff. There was no blood, no scorch marks, and no sign of battle, merely no people.

"You shouldn't have come," he muttered. "The whole point of this was to keep you safe."

She shook her head. "I'm not one of your students. You don't need to keep me safe."

"No, you're not one of the students. You're even more important to me." He drew his wand and cast a shield spell. "And I don't want you to endanger yourself. You already gave up something important to save me the first time."

Mara raised her hands and did the same. "You seem to forget that I'm the one who gives the orders."

"At the school, not here." He managed a slight smirk.

A wooden door in the back of the common room squeaked open, and the pale, light-haired man Raine had described stepped out, a wand in hand. Xander didn't recognize his face but he knew the ring, even from across the room.

"Sometimes, you have to see something up close to truly believe it," the newcomer declared with a grin. "I've been following you, but until now, I wasn't sure. I almost convinced myself it wasn't you."

"I have no idea who you are," he replied and raised his wand. "But I assume you killed Alfonso."

"You understand nothing." The man glanced at Mara. "This isn't your affair, Berens. I've no quarrel with you or your school. This is only about Xander. Leave."

"Do you expect me to walk away simply because you said that?" She scoffed.

"You don't understand," he muttered, a huge grin still on his face as if painted there. "You're supposed to be fall, Xander. Dead. Yet you're here, walking around and very much alive. It's not right. It's messed things up."

"Sorry." Xander shrugged. "Death didn't take. Why did you take Alfonso's ring? To send a message?"

"You still don't understand." The wizard laughed. "I have no choice." He pointed his wand and shouted a fireball spell. Mara threw her hand up. The flaming attack sped toward her companion, only to strike her conjured invisible wall. "You don't understand," the man screamed again.

Xander cast a restraining spell. Two thick chains hurtled toward their adversary, who swiped with his wand and whispered his own enchantment. The chains sizzled and turned into glass doves before they fell and shattered.

"Cute," he said and raised an eyebrow at their attacker.

"You don't have to fight," the wizard replied. "Just...give up."

Mara narrowed her eyes. A white-blue stun bolt erupted from her palm and struck the man to reveal a thick, shimmering shield that disappeared after a couple of seconds.

"You were supposed to die," he shouted and jerked his arm to point his wand up.

He grinned when the ceiling cracked and a piece gave way and plummeted. Xander cast a quick spell and flung the chunk at his opponent. It pounded into the shield, and the man backed away with a grunt. Xander didn't hesitate and launched a fireball. Mara held her palm out to pelt the wizard with stun bolts.

Their adversary fell to one knee. "It's not fair. You were supposed to be fall."

"What does that even mean?" Xander shouted. "You're the one who tried to kill me, and you killed Alfonso. Why?"

"I didn't kill him." The man smiled and cut through the air with his wand. Tables spun toward him and formed a swirling barrier against Mara's attack. She ceased rather than waste the effort. He layered another shield over himself. "What makes you think I killed Alfonso?"

"There's no way he would ever give up that ring." Xander backed away. They at least had the man on defense, and despite the grin on his face, his gaze darted constantly as if in nervousness.

"No, he wouldn't give up the ring."

Mara took a few deep breaths and raised both hands. Bright lines of white light arced between them. "I'll give you your chance. You'll know when."

Xander nodded and pointed his wand at the man as he began a complicated chant.

The wizard shook his head, still protected by the tables that swirled around him. "I'm more powerful now. Far more powerful than you realize, but I can't concentrate because you messed everything up. There's still a chance for you to be fall if I kill you here."

He flung his arm out with his wand and screamed another incantation. The wall behind Mara exploded in a shower of wood shards. The force of the explosion knocked her forward, and she hissed in pain before she released her own spell. Her bright bolt careened toward the man. It powered through the table and struck him in the chest. His shield flashed and dissipated.

The wizard catapulted into a wall. Xander took his chance and completed his spell. Wood peeled away from the wall in long strips before it transformed into nylon rope. It wound around his adversary's arms. His depleted shield didn't protect his wand, and one of the ropes snagged it and flung it to the other side of the room. He collapsed to his knees, still smiling.

"You could still be fall," he insisted.

Mara winced. There were several holes in the back of her shirt. "I knew I should have strengthened the shield." She twisted her arm to touch her back and murmured a quiet incantation. Her hand glowed for a moment as her wounds sealed.

Xander marched over to the captured wizard and

pointed his wand at his head. "You tried to kill me, and you tried to kill the woman I love. You killed Alfonso, too."

"She's not important," his prisoner muttered, his smile finally gone. "She's not fall. You're fall."

"It's over," Mara said softly. "We've won."

He kept his wand pointed at the man, his eyes narrowed as he took slow, even breaths. His lips parted slightly before he raised his wand and shook his head. "Whoever you are, you should never have come back."

Several kemana police rushed inside through the hole in the wall, their wands and swords at the ready. They paused, confusion on their faces when they saw Mara.

Xander snorted and nodded to the police. "This is a good time to answer a few questions."

CHAPTER TWENTY-TWO

The warded holding cell was unfurnished except for a single cot. Elaborate glyphs had been carved into every bar and along the floor and ceiling directly in front of the small room. A shimmering field stood between the occupant and the bars. The man knelt in the center and stared directly ahead, his eyes unfocused.

"It's over," Xander said as he paced in front of the bars. "Blowing up half a business and attempting to murder two professors from the School of Necessary Magic aren't exactly the kinds of things anyone looks on with approval around here. The Ruby Falls authorities will turn you over to the PDA. Your very short trial will probably end with you in an ultramax, given some of the magic you've used."

"Why are you here?" the pale man asked, his expression blank. "They took my ring."

"That's not your ring, and I'm here because Mara pulled some strings and I deserve to know who you are. The Ruby Falls police think I might even help them find out because they couldn't get the truth from you. They told me how whatever's going on with you messes up their truth spells."

The prisoner nodded slowly. "It does many things."

"It?"

"The curse."

"A curse? That's what this is about?" He glared at him. "You tried to kill me twice. You tried to kill Mara. You killed several people who might have been misguided but they used to be my friends. And I want to know why. I deserve to know why. I've defended my school, but it's not like I've spent the last couple of decades hunting members of the dark families."

The wizard turned his head slowly toward Xander and blinked as if he noticed him for the first time. "And why? I had no choice. That's why. It was the only path left to me."

"No choice?" Xander snarled. "No choice but to kill me? What's this even about? Because I turned my back on dark magic? That's what I don't understand about all of this. Killing me and Alfonso makes sense, but the others? Why? They weren't radicals like Alfonso, and they didn't turn their back on their past comrades like I did."

"The cause? Comrades?" The prisoner looked confused for a moment before his blank look returned. "You don't understand."

"Then make me understand. Somehow, this all goes back to Alfonso. You had his ring, after all."

The wizard shook his head. "I didn't kill Alfonso. I am Alfonso, even though I forget that myself at times."

He snorted. "You expect me to believe that? You only claim that because I can't use a truth spell on you. You killed him. You helped assassinate him because he was a radical."

"Shall I talk about everything we discussed in the past, Xander?" The man smiled. "About the strawberry-haired girl you once had a crush on when you first became a man, about how we both believed the opening of the gates would start in our lifetimes? How about that foolish Griffin DuBois? I remember what you said about them. 'The Griffins claim such morality, but how are they different than the dark families? They simply want to control everything.'"

Xander froze and his heart thundered. "It can't be. I saw you die."

Alfonso nodded. "I should have died there, but I was always prepared. I told you that. Remember what I used to say. 'If you die because you're surprised, you deserve to die.'" He laughed. "But they did surprise me, not only with an attack but a curse—a thorough curse, one that made me sleep for too long to seek proper vengeance, and while I slept, the curse ravaged me. My preparations weren't thorough enough." He shook his head. "Why couldn't you be fall like I needed? The others played their part. Winter, spring, and summer. The sacrifices were linked to you. They had to be. The removal won't work without fall. You can't have only three seasons."

He stared at the man in disbelief. "None of this had anything to do with me leaving that world behind, did it? It had nothing to do with anything but you trying to save your own life at the expense of others."

The prisoner shook his head, a disappointed expression on his face. "I told you. The strong should live. The weak should serve them. This is a way the weak can serve, and there's still a chance for you."

Xander turned his back on the man and snorted. "I don't know what curse they used on you, but it's obviously destroying your mind, too. Whatever curse is coming can take you, I'm not dying for you. I might have once, but you aren't that man anymore, and you've already killed people who hadn't even personally wronged you. I thought that was one line you wouldn't cross. I won't give up my life, not after I got Mara back." He headed toward the door. "Enjoy prison. Maybe they can find a cure."

"You can't walk away," Alfonso shrieked. "I'm the stronger man."

He put his hand on the door handle. "Maybe, but people are always stronger together. And that's why you lost." He opened the door and stepped out of the room to the shouts and cries of the captive.

Xander gulped down half his glass of wine. He sat across from Mara on the couch in her cottage. The newly opened bottle sat on the table, more a salve for a wounded soul than a victory elixir.

"The Passing of the Seasons," he explained. "Once I realized what he meant by fall, I was able to look it up as I vaguely remembered someone describing something like it back in my dark magic days. It's a vicious, vicious dark magical ritual. It involves four sacrifices in a slow and measured way, but at least one has to be someone you had an important connection with. It provides powerful healing or the removal of curses, but only if you're willing to turn your back on someone you supposedly care about."

"This is the perversion of dark magic." She sighed. "So he targeted you because you were friends? And the others? I thought you said he didn't know them."

"He didn't. They were collateral damage." He swirled his wine. "I won't claim they were innocent or good people in your sense of those words, but they didn't deserve to be fuel for some dying, insane wizard trying to cling to life after he'd miscalculated against his enemies." He frowned. "I suppose it's my fault."

"No, it's not. You didn't try to assassinate him the first time, and you didn't curse him. You also didn't force him to turn to such heinous dark magic. There are many wizards who can be blamed in this situation, but you're not on that list."

Xander thought that over. He wanted to believe the words, but if he hadn't allowed himself to be swallowed by the world of dark magic, he would never have had a connection to Alfonso that would have even made him a part of the ritual.

Mara frowned. "Why does he look different? You didn't recognize him. Did he change his appearance to hide?"

He shook his head. "No, actually that's a side-effect of the ritual, or maybe even a main effect. That's the problem. The ritual can help a wizard stay alive when he would have otherwise died from something like a powerful curse, but besides the sacrifices you need to help fuel the spell, it plays havoc with appearance and memory. It's almost like a partial rebirth." He finished his wine. "It's useless only for extending life, but it happens to be one of the few ways to beat certain extremely powerful curses. It might very well have been the only way he could keep himself alive."

She nodded. "So that's what happened? They cursed and attempted to murder him because of dark wizard politics?"

"As far as I can tell. The complication was the magic he used to survive the attack and that it didn't counteract the curse they used."

"But why a curse for someone you intend to kill?"

Xander shrugged. "Because they probably knew, on some level, that someone as smart as Alfonso would have a trick like the one he had prepared. They wanted to make sure he was dead, but the ritual he used is pure dark magic of the evilest kind." He frowned and refilled his glass. "So, it was a dark wizard plot like we guessed, but not the kind we thought. It was a man trying to save himself at the expense of others because of craven cowardice." He shook his head. "A man consumed by both the dark magic used on him and the dark magic used to save himself. I don't know when he woke up exactly, but he got desperate enough to use that ritual."

He sipped his wine. "I guess he thought he was out of options. I'd like to say I would never have done the same, but there was a time I was so lost in dark magic..." He chuckled. "We both know how that story ended. I want to hate him, but I can't help but pity him in the end."

"There's nothing wrong with that sentiment, but we shouldn't say he was out of options." Mara shook her head. "He had an option. He could have accepted his own death instead of trying to prolong it no matter the cost."

He managed a smile even as his stomach twisted itself

into knots. "I'm sorry, Mara. I don't know if it's better or worse that this was petty self-preservation versus a deep plot, but it doesn't change the fact that it was someone from my past. It's been decades now, and it keeps coming back."

"I made my choice when you were poisoned, and I made my choice more recently." She filled her own glass. "I understand your past, and I also accept that you've moved past it. At least now, the poisoning mystery is over."

"But this might not be the last time my past comes back." His eyebrows raised questioningly.

"I know," she said. "But if it comes back, we'll do what we did in this case. We'll put it to rest together."

CHAPTER TWENTY-THREE

Raine closed the huge book, *A Basic Overview of Etruscan Magical Practices*, and pushed it to the side of the table to join several other disappointments. With her focus on FBI training and Madelyn during the last couple of months, she had lacked the time to perform deep research on the symbol on Cina's necklace. She'd even forgotten about it for a while due to the limited number of kemana visits that semester and the fact that the woman hadn't approached her again after their first encounter. For a moment, she wondered if she had done something to offend her. Maybe she had expected more enthusiasm in the mystery of the symbol.

Whether she had offended her or not, the good news was that Madelyn had found new confidence and a new friend outside the Trouble Squad. That, along with a cryptic statement from Professor Powell that the situation Raine had indirectly stumbled into had been resolved, left a void in the mind of the mystery-obsessed teen. Identifying Cina's symbol was an interesting low-key way to sate her desire without disrupting her other studies or her time with her friends, and it didn't require her to risk her life or run around Charlottesville.

Head Librarian Decker chatted quietly to Joe at the front desk. She had almost asked him about the symbol but decided against it. This wasn't a conspiracy of dark wizards or a crazed chaos witch conspiring against the school. Reduced to its essence, it was a semi-bored student playing a game. And what fun was a game when you cheated?

She pulled her next book in front of her. It was a history book she had read before, *Magic in Western Europe During the Hidden Era*. She vaguely recalled seeing the symbol in the book, but she'd believed the same thing about five other books she had skimmed that week and ended up disappointed each time.

There was no reason to reread the text until she found the symbol, which made flipping through it a matter of minutes instead of hours. She exhaled a sigh, disappointed yet again, as she arrived at the last chapter. By now, she was convinced she had wasted more time than the secret deserved and it might be easier to track the woman down and demand that she explain the meaning. That didn't seem as cheap as asking Head Librarian Decker.

Raine turned a few more pages. Her breath caught as she stared at a small black and white drawing in the corner of the page. The depicted symbol was almost an exact match for the patterns on Cina's necklace. She ran her finger over it as she read the text, information she didn't actually remember reading. Perhaps she'd skipped it the first time she went through the book because of a momentary distraction.

The Eye of Thoth is the most common symbolic motif associated with the Children of Thoth. Despite the name's association with Egyptian mythology, all reliable records date the founding of the magical society to 742 A.D. in Constantinople.

An aggressive policy of recruitment helped the so-called Thothites increase the population of their local Thothite communities in addition to spreading them to other kemanas, but they only achieved major concentrations in Europe and Northern Africa. At their zenith in the eleventh century, the Thothites claimed membership in the high hundreds, but it has been impossible to confirm these numbers independently of potentially biased Thothite records.

Blurring the line between magical research society and cult, the Children of Thoth claimed proper training could allow a wizard or witch to tap into a primordial source of magic more fundamental than that of the magical energies of Oriceran or what is stored by the kemanas themselves. Although clear third-party documentation of impressive Thothite magical activity exists, the observed magic isn't inconsistent with access to artifacts and basic kemana magical storage despite the members' claims that they were able to transcend the limits on Earth-based magic associated with the then closed gates.

The Children of Thoth's continued public non-kemana use of magic created difficulties for the magical authorities, who were doing their best to conceal the presence of active magicals in the cities near the kemanas. It was this disregard for magical secrecy that led to the downfall of the Thothites. Crackdowns created difficulties for further recruitment and eventually caused almost all formal Thothite-affiliated groups in kemanas to diminish.

Today, small pockets of Thothites remain, but the modern groups function more as mutual-aid societies with an overly elaborate emphasis on ritual. The use of religious terminology and secrecy has led to some accusations of cult-like behavior but given that the group's primary crime was in the open use of magic, modern authorities have had little reason to persecute the group.

Modern Thothites don't deny some of the most outrageous ancient claims concerning magical power, but they insist that their ideological ancestors might have had access to alternative magical techniques that while not truly revolutionary, might still have been useful if not suppressed.

The head librarian wandered over to Raine. "What has your attention today?"

"The Children of Thoth."

The gnome's eyebrows raised. "Thothites? I haven't heard anyone mention them in a long time, and they have always been restricted to Earth. They never had a presence on Oriceran."

She tapped the picture of the symbol. "I think there are Thothites in the kemana."

"Really now? Interesting. I've not been there as much these last few months." Head Librarian Decker tilted his head to skim the passage. "This description of them is accurate." He shrugged. "They were an interesting group, but their claims that they'd accessed some kind of deeper magic were absurd. While it's not as if there is nothing new to learn about magic, it's important to remember full and open magic never went away on Oriceran."

"But that might be a reason why Oricerans never developed something like what the Thothites claimed. If they didn't need another source of magic, there was no reason to go looking for one."

An unusual expression suffused the gnome's face—surprise. His poppy blew a raspberry before the gnome nodded. "That's a good point, but you can flip it around to magicals on Earth. If the magical authorities thought they had a useful technique that would not rely on magic flowing from Oriceran, they would have made use of it. Despite the fact that many people often act as if Oriceran and Earth magicals act in concert, it's not the case that every magical on Oriceran cooperates. Obeying the Great Treaty isn't the same thing as being true allies."

"Huh," Raine said. "That makes sense. So the Children of Thoth were liars? Then and now?"

He sighed. "It's not fraud if you honestly believe it, and everything I've seen of the Thothites suggests they honestly believed they'd found something. It's a sad delusion in that sense. I will note in the documented cases I've heard of that all they'd done was stumble onto a few artifacts that enhanced their magic and convinced themselves they'd found some way to get around the fundamental restrictions of magic." He shook his head. "Just as deluded human engineers continue to insist they can make perpetual energy machines, there are magicals who think there is some infinite source of magical power they can access with enough research or dedication. Magic might be powerful and can accomplish effects that many humans find miraculous, but it still has its limits. Such is the nature of its existence."

She pointed to the symbol. "There's a woman in the kemana who has a pendant with this symbol. She wouldn't tell me what it meant. I wonder if she's a Thothite with a magical enhancement artifact."

"That's likely. It's interesting that the Thothites are being secretive in Ruby Falls." He chuckled. "But I suspect that many of the modern adherents are more interested in the trappings of being a secret society than actually studying advanced magic. The Children of Thoth aren't the only group who were something far more in the past than they are in modern times but be cautious anyway. Those who claim a direct connection to ancient traditions can oftentimes be arrogant."

"I don't know what to make of Cina. That's the woman with the pendant. She seemed very nice, but she also was obviously playing a game with me by forcing me to study this to figure it out." Raine closed the book. "I'm not interested in becoming a Thothite, but I'm interested in finding out what she thinks she's hiding."

"Not all apparent mysteries are truly that." Head Librarian Decker smiled and glanced at a ladder moving along the stacks with no one near it. "Hmm. It's time for a small tuning. If you'll excuse me, Raine, I need to handle this."

"No problem." She waved.

The gnome headed toward the rogue ladder and the flower on his bowler growled the entire time.

Raine looked at the book once again. She had her answer, but it only led to more questions and more mysteries. Still, at least it didn't sound like anything dangerous. Her smile slowly faded.

Something was bothering her, something on the edge of her conscious mind. It might be her looking for trouble, but she had long since learned to trust her instincts, and it was time for some instincts to lead her to evidence.

"I'll have to be careful about this, but I definitely need to look into Cina," she murmured.

CHAPTER TWENTY-FOUR

Raine peeked around the corner of the gleaming white walls of the kemana jeweler. "I haven't seen her yet."

Cameron frowned from behind her. "You said you wanted to go on a date, and after dinner, all we've done is look for Cina. This isn't a date. This is a case."

"Dinner and an activity together constitute a date." She grinned. "Would you have preferred that I looked for her by myself? I can already see it." She mock-glared and lowered her voice in her best Cameron impression. "I need to protect you, and I can't protect you if you run off and get yourself in trouble without telling me."

He grunted. "I don't sound like that, but even if I do, that's right. At best, this woman is weird, and you also admit you think there might be something more there."

Raine flashed him a challenging look. "Oh, so you trust my suspicions now?"

"When it involves you wandering around the kemana

not even sure what you're doing, I have to." He shrugged. "And something's always rubbed me the wrong way about the woman."

She stepped around the corner and walked down the street with a sigh. "You know what I realized?"

"I'm an awesome boyfriend?"

"I already knew that." She smiled. "No, I'm making this Cina thing too hard. I'm not trying to actually sneak up on her, so I should simply ask. How hard can it be to find a woman wandering around in a white robe with a silver pendant? That's unusual even by the kemana standards."

"And what do you plan to do when you find her? You're not exactly close."

"Nothing special. I'll simply ask her if she's in the Children of Thoth." Raine shrugged. "It's not exactly a secret society."

"And if she denies it? What then? Will you accuse her of lying?"

"No, I'll figure something out. A simple lie can't stop an investigation."

"So it's an investigation now?"

"Sure." She gestured down the street. "We're investigating someone so it is, by definition, an investigation, right?"

The shifter folded his arms. "We were supposed to be on a date."

"An investigative date."

"Let's ask someone about her and be done with it."

"Agreed." She marched across the street toward a street vendor selling red frosted rolls from a small hand-pulled wooden cart. He was a newer vendor. She had seen him for the first time about a month prior, but she'd never purchased his food. "Excuse me, sir."

"Would you like a roll, young lady?" he asked with a bright smile. "Delicious. Family recipe. All non-magical ingredients if you're on one of those trendy diets."

Raine fished a few Ruby Falls coins out of her pockets and handed them to him. "Two please."

The vendor scooped up two rolls with white napkins and handed them over. "Please enjoy."

"I'm sure we will." She smiled at him. "You wouldn't have happened to have seen Cina around today?"

He frowned, a little bewildered. "Cina? Who is that?"

"She's a beautiful woman in a white robe with a silver necklace and long brown hair. She has a really nice smile."

Recognition flashed on the man's face. "I didn't know her name, but yes, I've seen her around." He pointed down the street. "She passed that way about an hour ago. She was talking to a Kilomea last time I saw her."

"Thanks." She took a bite out of the sweet roll, waved, and wandered down the street while she glanced at some of the nearby shops. Most had open windows. There were many potential witnesses. Tracking Cina down was now merely a matter of time.

Cameron scarfed his roll down in a few quick bites. He swallowed. "This beats simply walking around hoping we see her."

She took another bite of her roll. "If this is an investigation, it's time to interview more witnesses."

Thirty minutes and four witnesses later, Raine jogged past several restaurants toward the white-robed form in the distance. Cameron remained at her side and glanced behind them on occasion to confirm they weren't being followed.

She swallowed. The woman might have actively avoided her, and she had no plan if her quarry simply decided to leave. If she ran, pursuit might come off as overly aggressive. If she were a Thothite, she might even have a natural wariness that came from a history of oppression.

Cina didn't run away. Instead, she stopped and waited for her to arrive.

"Hello, Cina," she said.

The woman smiled. "Hello again, Raine. It's been a long time since we last talked. I suppose that's my fault."

"It's not a big deal." She looked around and leaned in to whisper, "Your pendant. It's the Eye of Thoth."

The woman's delicate eyebrows rose. "Yes, it is. It's not exactly a huge secret, but I've found it encouraging that a little extra effort can help me find people truly interested in what I might have to say."

"You're a member of the Children of Thoth, then?"

Cina nodded slowly. "Yes, I am. I've been involved with them for a while now."

Cameron frowned. "Why all the secrecy then? It's not like it's illegal to be a member of the group. At least that's what Raine told me."

"No, it's not illegal, but those who are aware of the history of our group often have misconceptions. I've personally found that if people get to know me before they understand I'm a priestess in the Children of Thoth, they'll be more open-minded about what I have to say and won't prematurely judge me or my friends."

"You're a priestess?" he asked and suspicion colored his face.

"It's more of a ceremonial title than anything," Cina said with a shrug. "Our group is mostly about spreading our magical ideals at this point." She sighed. "Now that the gates have begun to open, we have a chance to spread them again, and we do feel our ideals could be helpful to all magicals, both those from Earth and Oriceran,"

"And what specifically are those ideals?" Raine asked. "I've read about your group in books and talked to a few people, but much of that was about the past so it's not clear to me what you actually believe."

The woman took a deep breath. "Of course, I would love to talk to anyone curious about the Children of Thoth, if only to be a friend, but it would take time, and you aren't the only one with questions. In the interests of efficiency, maybe you could come to a meeting where we talk about these things, along with other people interested."

"Other people?"

Cina nodded. "Of course. As I said, we have ideals and an approach to magic that could be helpful to many people provided they have an open mind."

"When are you meeting?" she asked.

"We're meeting next Saturday. Do you know the blue building near that lovely dress store and the potions shop run by that gnome?" Cina pointed. "It's several miles in that direction."

Raine nodded. "I know exactly where that is. I've walked past it several times."

"We would love to see you there." She smiled and looked at Cameron. "Our emphasis is on magic, but we don't object to shifters coming. Like I said, the Thothites could always use more allies, regardless of their magical abilities."

He narrowed his eyes. "How did you know I was a shifter? I never told you that."

There was a hint of mischief in her eyes. "You might have asked about me, but I asked about Raine and all her friends. It's always good to know more about your neighbors." She waved. "I hate to run off so quickly, but there is a gentleman I need to speak to soon."

She waved in response. "Thank you for your time, Cina. I'll see you at the meeting."

Cameron offered a nod. Cina walked away, a warm smile on her face and with no hint of any concern or tension.

Raine waited until the woman was about thirty yards away before she spoke. "I wonder if I was wrong about her avoiding me before. She seemed very happy to invite both of us. I can't be sure. My instincts tell me there is more here than I see, but maybe I simply want there to be."

He frowned. "I don't know. I get a bad vibe from her. And she's not only some random Thothite. She's a priestess. It's a little cultish. You don't have to be an FBI trainee to find that suspicious."

She shrugged. "That's even more of a reason for us to go."

"Why do you think that?" The shifter glanced at the now distant Cina and back to Raine. "Unless you've been lying to me for years, I can't see you joining a cult."

"If they are up to no good and tricking people, then don't we have a duty to check into it?" She placed her hands on her hips and raised her chin, her face defiant.

Cameron's frown flowed into a smirk. "I thought this was only about you satisfying yourself with a mystery, but now, you're talking about duty? You're not an FBI agent yet. You're a student. Your only real duty is to do well at school."

"Helping people is the duty of everyone, not only law enforcement." She summoned her stubborn face. Her boyfriend tended to fold quicker when she used it. She didn't like using the weapon, but she needed to make it clear she wouldn't let this go. A quiet sigh followed. "It's like I said. My instincts. Yours, too. I'm not sure what the deal is with the Children of Thoth, but I can't say I'm not somewhat suspicious of Cina. The level of secrecy doesn't make sense on first examination, but on the other hand, she's fine with some random students coming to her meeting." She nodded at him. "And she wants you to come, even knowing you're a shifter. That's a piece of evidence that she's not as dangerous as either of us think."

"Her checking us out is a little weird." He shrugged. "But if she's not lying, I suppose that makes sense."

"If anything weird happens, we'll leave right away. How does that sound?"

"So our date today was tracking her down." He chuckled. "And we'll spend a perfectly good date day at something that, at best, might be a gathering of some weird group that believes they have special magic and at worst, might be a cult?"

"Yes." She nodded cheerfully. "That sounds like an interesting date."

CHAPTER TWENTY-FIVE

Even though early December had greeted the area with crisp, clear skies, the temperature continued to dip as the end of fall prepared for the beginning of winter, but it was still far from firebug candy weather. Raine rubbed her chilled hands together as she strolled out of the front door of the main mansion. Her breath emerged in short, visible puffs.

It wasn't a casual stroll. She needed to find a few plants for the final potions project of the semester. Even though they still had a couple of weeks left before they began the brewing, she thought finding the ingredients while the weather remained nice made more sense than scrambling during the last few days like half the class, especially if it was raining or snowing.

A few minutes of walking brought her near the stables. Riding had been one of the major sacrifices of her increased focus on FBI training. While she had visited him a few times, she hadn't ridden Storm once that semester.

She sighed. While she understood life always required

trade-offs, and she understood her future path would constrain her time even more, that didn't mean she never longed for more time to do everything she enjoyed. Juggling school, a boyfriend, and FBI training had proved harder than she expected—difficult but rewarding.

"I'll have to take Storm out for a decent ride before vacation," she murmured. "But I can't complain too much when I spend my weekends investigating the Children of Thoth." She wasn't sure if she would be more annoyed or happy if she found out there was nothing more to the Thothites than an overly enthusiastic leader who liked to play at being coy. It wasn't like Cina had denied her pendant was an artifact, and no one had anything too bad to say about them other than they found the woman and a few of her friends a little strange.

Raine hadn't run into any of the other Thothites to the best of her knowledge, but perhaps they didn't wear the Eye of Thoth. She stopped and blinked. While she'd asked around a little more about recruitment, most people weren't interested. They all said the members seemed nice but they assumed their pitch would end with a request for money.

White and silver in the distance caught Raine's attention. Dorvu flew low near a patch of grass along the entrance to the forest A thin, roughly circular layer of ice sat on top of the grass. The silver dragon circled the area, his mouth open, and a stream of frigid, white breath poured out and added to the ice. He finished after a few passes and landed at the edge to rest on his haunches.

The dragon distracted her, so she didn't initially notice the smiling Madelyn standing near him. The Coral Elf stepped away from the dragon and walked along the edge of the ice patch, her hands raised. Faint magic filled the air as the ice smoothed visibly. After a minute of effort, a now perfect circle of several inches of ice lay there.

Raine jogged toward the two of them, now understanding what they were doing. "Isn't it still a little warm for an ice rink?"

Dorvu raised his head, a hint of haughty pride in his eyes. "It'll last long enough, and it won't take long to create a new one."

Madelyn nodded. "I ran into Dorvu. We were talking, and I asked him about it."

"Why the sudden interest in ice rinks?" she asked.

"I was talking with Erin about fun and ice a few days ago, and she mentioned how Dorvu's good at this kind of thing. I was so afraid of him last year, I never even knew." She smiled at the dragon. "Thank you again."

Erin was the girl Madelyn had saved on Halloween. They'd spent a lot of time together in November, and Raine was happy the elf had made another friend and had come out of her shell more. Erin also had more time to spend with her than anyone in the FBI Trouble Squad.

Dorvu raised his wings. With a few mighty flaps, he rose into the sky. "You're welcome." He headed higher and circled as he ascended before he soared over the treetops and frosted a few on the way.

Raine stuck her hands in her jacket pockets. "Don't you need skates?" She looked around but didn't see any. "I could make something half-way decent, but they won't be great."

The girl shook her head, stepped onto the ice, and

smiled. Thin blades of glowing ice coalesced from the bottom of her lace-up boots. She stretched her arms to either side. "This is something I've wanted to try since we watched *Arpak on Ice* at movie night. It looked both beautiful and fun."

Raine was surprised that Adrien, of all people, had brought a slapstick comedy about a figure-skating Arpak to movie night. No one could remember ever seeing Madelyn laugh so much.

"You'll do an octuple lutz with the help of wings?" she asked and grinned. "That would be impressive."

Madelyn pumped her legs and launched herself forward. Her smooth movement was impressive. It was like she had skated for years.

"Is this your first time?" Raine asked. "You look like you're having a good time."

The elf nodded, her pale face red from the touch of the cold air. She turned with ease and lifted one leg behind her before she spread her arms out. "Yes. I didn't think about doing this kind of thing before. It seemed kind of silly when Vianna and I were still trying to stabilize, and I didn't know about all the fun things out there. I wouldn't have tried to ask her even if I knew, though. I was...scared all the time. It consumed me."

"And now?"

She looked thoughtful as she turned. "It's always there —the fear—but now, I can push it off and concentrate on things that don't scare me."

"I'm so happy to see you out here having fun. You seem so much happier since the beginning of the semester."

Madelyn sighed. "I'll be honest. It's easy to do this

around Dorvu or you and Erin." She attempted a jump but tripped on the landing. Quickly, she thrust her hand out and hands of ice grew from the rink to catch her.

Raine grimaced. "Are you okay?"

The ice hands retreated into the rink as Madelyn stood. She giggled. "I guess it's harder when you don't have wings."

She laughed. "Wings might help."

Madelyn managed a graceful spin. She pulled her arms in to speed up. Despite her fall, she looked like she had been born on ice.

Raine's first time ice skating had involved far more falls and an aching tail bone. She winced at the memory.

The elf stopped after spinning three times, her wrists crossed above her. "This feels...good. Very good." Uncertainty flavored her voice.

"You're very good at it," Raine said. "You have natural talent. I wonder if that comes with the Coral Elf connection to water and ice."

Madelyn lowered her arms, her brow furrowed. "But I'm not a real Coral Elf."

She shook her head. "We've already been over this."

"I know." The girl sighed. "Erin tells me that, too."

"Then you should listen to her." She gestured to the ice. "And you shouldn't worry so much about what you think is real. Listen to the people who care about you."

Madelyn managed a small smile and skated toward the edge of the rink. "I would have never been able to try something like this if it wasn't for all of you." She took a deep breath. "Is it strange that I find skating so relaxing?"

Raine shook her head. "We all have special things that

appeal to us." She smiled. "You've said before that you don't always trust your words. Maybe moving like this is a way for you to express yourself without words, and you have such obvious natural talent. You should look into figure skating or ice dancing."

The elf turned, stopped, and sent a stream of shredded ice into the air. "Really?"

She nodded. "Everyone needs hobbies. Sometimes, those hobbies become a true passion like Sara's painting, or sometimes, they simply remain something fun and enjoyable, like Evie's baking."

"What's your hobby?"

Raine glanced at the stables in the distance. "Besides reading?

Madelyn nodded.

"It used to be riding, but these days, I guess you could say it's solving mysteries." She laughed and shrugged.

The elf stepped off the ice, her finger pointed at her feet. Her ice blades melted. "I like learning things, but I don't think I like mysteries I have to solve in real life." She nibbled her lip and looked over her shoulder at the ice rink. "I think I will look into figure skating. One thing I've realized these last few months is that it's okay that I'm still scared of most people, but I have friends, and it's okay to want more than simply to exist." She smiled and looked at the ground. "Thank you, Raine. For everything. I know I upset you when we first met, but it's because you have helped me that I've been able to adjust. I'm still scared, but I feel happy, too."

"You're welcome. And don't worry about what

happened before. I understand. I'm happy that you're adjusting to life at the School of Necessary Magic."

Madelyn rushed over to her and pulled her into a hug. "Thank you. No one can fully replace Vianna, but I feel like you're my new big sister."

She hugged the girl in return and stroked her hair. "I'm glad I could help."

CHAPTER TWENTY-SIX

Cameron sighed as he and Raine sat in two of the wooden chairs in the center of the modest room. Both chairs were in the front row. The Thothites obviously hadn't expected a huge crowd, as they'd only set up twenty seats. For some reason, none of the other attendees sat in the front row. About a dozen other people attended the meeting, all wizards or witches given the presence of wand holsters or loops and obvious Oriceran appearances. The priestess might want to reach out to Oricerans, but her message hadn't resonated, apparently. The other people murmured among themselves and ignored Cameron and Raine.

Cina hadn't yet stepped into the room. When they had arrived, they were led through a small hallway to the simple meeting room. Other than the chairs, there was a small black table at the front. There wasn't anything on it.

The shifter leaned over and whispered, "Are you sure about this? It's not too late to walk away, and we can still have a fun Saturday."

She shook her head. "I'm genuinely curious."

He looked over his shoulder. "We're the youngest ones here." He smirked. "I wonder what that says about us."

"It says I can't let things go, and it says you won't ever let me go where you think I might be in danger on my own." She grinned. "Thank you. I appreciate it."

The murmuring crowd quieted as Cina stepped into the room with a bright smile. She offered the crowd a nod and her gaze lingered on the two of them before she moved behind the table, her hands clasped in front of her.

"Thank you very much for attending this meeting today," she said, her voice soft. "I've spoken to each of you individually to personally extend you an invitation, so know that I'm pleased you would sacrifice your time to hear my message. Some of my associates will bring refreshments for after my discussion."

Raine folded her hands in front of her and waited.

Cina pulled her wand out to summon an image of Oriceran and Earth to float in front of her. She looked at Raine. "Some of you are too young to remember a time when the gates were closed." Her gaze shifted to one of the wizards toward the back. "Others remember a time when magic had to be kept secret, and that secrecy was fiercely maintained by different groups. There were arguably good reasons for that but now, the gates are open, and this represents an opportunity."

"What kind of opportunity?" a frowning wizard called.

"An opportunity for both Earth and Oriceran to advance beyond our pasts." Cina smiled, moved her wand again, and whispered. The image changed to shadowy forms gathered in a circle. "Everyone is so excited about the gates beginning to open, they forget the implications of the past."

"And what are those?" Raine asked. She watched carefully, curiosity alight in her face like it was for any lecture.

"What opens can close again." The image changed from the shadow figures to a stylized silver gate set in a stone wall. It slammed shut.

A sleepy-looking witch in the second row chuckled. "That won't be for thousands of years. Why should we care about what happens in thousands of years?"

"Because we have a duty to the future," Cina said. The image shifted to packed crystal spires that stretched into the sky. "But it goes beyond that. We of the Children of Thoth believe that much of the magical conflict that has afflicted the worlds is because of the inequities in power, based fundamentally on the perceived limits of magic. This has also created an underlying tension between Earth and Oriceran, as the Oricerans have always had full access to magic, whereas Earth has had to worry about the closing of the gates. But what if we could stop that? What if we could reach past these limitations to ensure Earth will never lack magic, not only in the future but to strengthen things now?"

"So this is about power, then?" Cameron asked, his tone skeptical.

Cina shook her head. "This is about making sure everyone has the same access to magic. That way, we all have the maximum potential to develop ourselves, and isn't that what everyone desires? Fulfilled potential? We of the Children of Thoth firmly believe that by increasing the potential of others, they can grow into someone better. It is their longing that compels them toward harmful acts." She smiled. "Today, you are all taking your first step on a journey that others have already started. Although we still have many steps left on our journey, together, we can reach the desired destination not only for ourselves but for everyone on Earth and Oriceran."

The image shifted to an orb that glowed with power.

"We of the Children of Thoth seek the source of the true magic," Cina explained. "A source of magic that goes beyond Oriceran or Earth individually and doesn't rely on the condition of gates that no one can control."

"And what is that source?" Cameron asked. "I've never heard anything to suggest something like that exists."

"We'll get to that eventually when the time is right, but first, let's talk more about the balance of magic between Earth and Oriceran."

The speech continued for thirty minutes and people asked the occasional question. While Cina smiled and was pleasant throughout, she constantly returned to the same themes of balancing magic and freeing both individuals and the planets from the limits of the magic with a continued emphasis on bringing equity of power to Earth magicals. She also avoided any specific details on how the Thothites intended to accomplish this lofty goal. Although there was the occasional question from the other attendees, no one seemed much interested in probing the finer details of how the Thothites intended to accomplish anything.

At the end of the speech, several of the attendees departed immediately, and the others didn't seem interested in talking to Cina as much as some of the cheese, fruit, and drinks brought in by the other members.

Raine took note of the two men and women who had carried the refreshment trays. They didn't wear white robes or pendants. They looked like anyone else she might see in Charlottesville, let alone the kemana. One man's sleeve rode up for a moment to reveal a tattoo of the Eye of Thoth on the back of his wrist.

"So what's the plan?" Cameron whispered.

"I should go talk to her," she whispered back.

He shrugged. "You do that. I'll get some cheese."

They stood and headed toward their respective targets. Cina finished chatting quietly to one of the other Thothites and offered Raine a bright smile.

"Thank you again for coming, Raine," Cina said. "I hope you found it enlightening."

"It was...interesting." She licked her lips. "But there were things I didn't understand."

"Oh? Feel free to ask anything you want." The woman gestured to the other members. They nodded and headed into the hall.

"I understand the goals of your plan, but it's unclear how you'll actually accomplish it."

Cina looked confused. "Really? I thought I made that clear. We'll achieve our plan by reaching for a more fundamental source of magic."

"Yes, you did say that." She took a deep breath. While she needed more information, she didn't want to appear too aggressive. She regretted not having Cameron nearby to provide Bad Cop cover for her Good Cop. "But I don't understand what that actually means. When we study spells or potions at the school, it's always a lot more detailed, and even for the magic we can't do yet—things like portals—they explain the mechanics. I need a little more concrete magical detail, is all."

Cina nodded slowly, an appraising look in her eyes. "I see." She leaned closer, an almost mischievous smile on her face. "You have a curious mind, something I think is a good thing, but this isn't the place for that kind of discussion. At least not yet. I'd suggest you come back for another meeting. This particular event was never intended to be anything more than an introductory discussion to introduce you to the most basic of Thothite beliefs."

"Are you saying I need to come back if I want any specific answers?" Raine tried her best to keep any obvious suspicion out of her voice, but she only partially succeeded.

"All knowledge needs to be placed in the proper context," the woman replied. "It's irresponsible to offer it otherwise, but I do encourage you to come back when we have our meeting next week. We'll have far fewer people, I suspect, and we'll go more in-depth."

She sighed. "I can't get any other information right now?"

"No, I'm sorry. I have to leave very soon, so I don't have time to provide a full explanation." Cina glanced at Cameron. "Since you're already bringing friends along, maybe you should consider bringing others—such as that Coral Elf girl I saw you with and her sister."

Raine blinked. "Madelyn? And Vianna…" She shook her head. "Vianna passed away last spring."

"Oh?" The priestess looked taken aback. "I'm sorry. I didn't realize that."

"You knew Madelyn had a sister, though? I'm surprised. I definitely don't remember seeing you around the kemana when Vianna was still alive, and you're kind of hard to miss."

"Of course. I didn't see her sister." Cina nodded. "I've heard people describe them. Two Coral Elves stand out, even in a place like this. They merely failed to mention her sister was dead."

"Madelyn isn't all that fond of meeting new people," Raine said. "I don't know if she would enjoy this kind of thing."

"Oh, that's unfortunate." She smiled. "I would strongly encourage you to bring her. She might find she has far more in common with us than perhaps some of the students at your school. You wouldn't want her to miss out on an opportunity, would you?"

"More in common with you as a Coral Elf?" She didn't bother to keep the doubt off her face or out of her voice. She didn't feel a need to clarify Madelyn's background and remained interested in why Cina would think an apparent Oriceran would be so much more receptive to a pitch that, by implication, emphasized bringing Earth magic to parity or greater. "I'm surprised you would want her to come. I thought you wanted to screen people before talking to them."

"Of course. But I trust in your judgment, Raine, and I know that any of your friends would be interested in our message, but I really must get going. We'll talk again more at our next meeting." Without even waiting for a response, she headed toward the hallway.

Raine glanced at Cameron who munched on cheese and fruit, then back to the departing Cina. "Why is she so interested in meeting Madelyn?" she murmured.

CHAPTER TWENTY-SEVEN

Madelyn sighed and folded her arms. She sat on the edge of her bed as her friend told her about the Thothite meeting in detail and Cina's personal request for her to attend.

"And that's it." Raine shrugged as she paced. "My instincts tell me there's something here, but it might simply be a delusional woman who thinks she can gain special magic power before the gates are fully open. She should probably take a vacation to Oriceran, but I have a feeling she wouldn't like it if I suggested it."

"What do you think about me going, Raine?" the girl asked.

"Are you interested in them as friends?"

She shook her head. "No. I have enough friends between you, Erin, and the others, but I want to help you if you need it."

"I don't know. There's something off here." Raine sighed. "I wish I could say what, but this might be a situation where evidence leads the case, but instincts lead to evidence."

"You think so?" Madelyn seemed tense and a trace of fear crept onto her face. "You don't think Cina is who she says she is?"

"I don't know, but I do think Cameron was right when he said they acted a little cult-like." She managed to stop pacing but tapped her foot instead. "And I didn't like how she refused to give me any specific answers. It felt like a sales pitch—all promises but with no clear indication of how those promises would be delivered." She frowned, her doubts mirrored on her face. "I don't think they're trying anything truly evil, but I do think there's a con somewhere in this. I haven't found the angle, though. I also don't understand why they would care to target students. Arguably, it's easier to con younger people, but there are too many downsides. We'll have less money and are more likely to go to authorities, either at the school or in the kemana."

The Coral Elf nodded. "Will you talk to anyone about the Children of Thoth?"

Raine shook her head. "Not yet. I like to trust my instincts, but there's still a strong possibility I'm wrong. Many people already don't trust Thothites because of their history, and if they aren't actually doing anything wrong, I would hate for them to be harassed because I'm suspicious. Hurting innocent people in pursuit of justice makes a mockery of justice."

"Then I should go to their next meeting." The girl nodded, a determined look on her face.

"Really?"

"Yes. You need to gather more evidence, right? If you bring me along, maybe this Cina will let her guard down and she'll admit what this is about. Then you don't have to feel bad when you ask the authorities to look into them." She rubbed the back of her neck, uncertainty on her face. "That's how it works in the movies I've seen and the books I've read anyway."

Raine took a deep breath. "It's not a bad plan, but I'm surprised that you want to do this."

Madelyn looked down and sighed. "Helping Erin at Halloween has given me confidence, but I wouldn't have even had enough for that if it weren't for you. I owe you, and this is a way I can pay you back. Even if it turns out to be nothing, at least you won't worry as much, and you'll feel better then. And I don't want one of my friends to worry."

"You're not wrong. The more I seem interested and willing to listen, the more she'll think I'm ready to agree to whatever scheme she has. Assuming she has a scheme." She snorted. "This is probably only a more sophisticated version of Hap's multi-level marketing scam. Maybe they need students so they can have distribution inside the school." She rubbed her cheek as she tried to imagine what kind of product they might be selling—perhaps a potion they claimed enhanced magic ability?

The elf tilted her head, confused. "Hap as in the ferret herbalist?"

Raine shook her head. "Don't worry about him. That said, we can't pretend there's no danger. If they are con artists, they might be willing to get a little rough."

"How dangerous can sitting in a room be?" Madelyn

rubbed her wrist and the fear infiltrated her face even though she tried to keep it out of her voice.

"Maybe not dangerous at all, but if we do this, I might as well bring everyone to make sure we have backup." She shrugged. "Cina claimed she trusted my judgment. There's no way she can complain if I bring more people." She smiled and the excitement kicked her heart rate up. "And you're one hundred percent sure about this? I don't want to do anything that upsets you."

Madelyn nodded. "I trust you, Raine, and I want to help you."

She smiled. "Then as an honorary member of our FBI Trouble Squad, you might help us capture some con artists."

"And if it turns out to only be a strange group with strange beliefs?"

Raine shrugged. "Then we'll know so we can help them find people who might actually be interested in what they have to say."

CHAPTER TWENTY-EIGHT

Cina smiled warmly and spread her arms in front of her. Raine and her friends filled the small number of chairs set up in the building. None of the other witches or wizards who attended the first meeting had returned, which conveniently meant everyone had somewhere to sit while the Thothite priestess delivered her short speech.

"To reiterate," she said at the end, "we of the Children of Thoth believe there is a primordial source of magic deeper than anything associated with Oriceran and with the appropriately applied rituals, it is possible to access that source of power now. We also believe—but have no proof, I'll admit—that in the past, magical authorities were also aware of this but chose to suppress this knowledge."

Adrien snorted. "Why would they do that?"

"Why did they hide magic, to begin with?" She sighed. "We have all heard the reasons, but don't they all seem self-serving? It's not as if magic was impossible on Earth when the gates were closed. They could prove the existence of magic simply by doing it in public, but instead, they chose to suppress groups like ours who did that. What did it achieve? Are we a better world today because the truth of magic was hidden? Does anyone think it would have been worse for everyone to know the truth?"

"But if everyone knew about magic, they might have hunted magicals." William frowned. "There would have been danger. People were more suspicious and less likely to tolerate differences."

"There was more danger than in the age of technology? I doubt that. The reality is magicals were far safer in the past by virtue of their abilities." Cina shook her head. "Don't let revisionist history lead you away from the obvious. All deceit is poisonous at its heart, and people lied for thousands of years for mostly self-serving reasons. They complain now of chaos, but it's because they allowed deceit to guide their actions in the past that this very chaos exists." She sighed. "I understand that the men and women who did this bore no ill will in their hearts. They meant well, but I would strongly argue that they were misguided and did harm to the magical communities of Earth in the long run—harm that we can now ameliorate if we work hard."

Raine frowned. Despite the woman's promises of more details, it was hard to miss the fact that in her speech and her follow-up, she hadn't presented any concrete information other than vague references to rituals to achieve her espoused goals. It all sounded very exciting, but without an actual explanation, it was difficult to determine if it was possible.

Madelyn sat quietly beside her. She hadn't said anything the entire time and instead, she constantly rubbed her armrests and nibbled her lip. Her earlier bravado seemed like a distant memory, and Raine regretted agreeing to it, even if she was proud of how the girl wanted to help. Being brave in the confines of her room or school was a far different matter than facing others in Ruby Falls.

Cameron folded his arms. "You argue that they had access to super-magic in the past, but they purposefully didn't use it? That doesn't seem likely. Nobody sets aside a weapon they can use unless the other person has the same weapon."

"How painfully cynical, but the truth is it's hard to suppress knowledge if you constantly flaunt it," Cina countered. "The magical status quo satisfied their needs, so they found it sufficient. Why risk it, from their perspective?"

"And how exactly do you plan to access this power?" Sara asked. "You mentioned a ritual, but what kind of ritual? How exactly does it work? What does it need?"

"You have to understand there are a few secrets we still have to keep until people fully commit to becoming a Thothite." The priestess smiled. "And I know none of you are ready for that. Your presence here is welcome, but some additional meetings, discussions, and time with us are necessary before we share our innermost secrets."

Raine narrowed her eyes. "Wait. You claim you can already access this magic now? The primordial magic as you call it? Can't you at least demonstrate how it works?"

The woman assumed a regretful expression. "Doing so will create attention I don't want to bring to my group until we're sure about new members. It would be dangerous."

"Why is it dangerous?" Evie asked. "Are you saying this magic could hurt us?"

"I'm not saying that." She glanced at each of the gathered students. "But there might be those who come to take our knowledge without accepting the responsibility that comes with it. I won't lie to you. We've been forced to leave other areas because of such oppression."

Adrien shook his head. "That was a long time ago."

"No, I'm talking about in modern times. It's why we don't have any permanent roots."

"Wait, how is this supposed to bring peace and stuff if it causes trouble?" Philip frowned and didn't bother to hide his skepticism. "Something doesn't add up here."

"We merely need to recruit a critical mass of people," Cina said and her smile looked forced for the first time since Raine had met her. "If they believe what we believe and have access to our abilities, it won't matter if some would seek to harass us. I'm not claiming this is a project that will be complete in mere years. Decades might be required, even centuries, but that's still a small sacrifice compared to the eventual closing of the gates and thousands of years of imbalance again."

She took a deep breath and closed her eyes. When she re-opened them, her more typical bright and warm smile had returned. "This is why we have to proceed carefully in who we want to recruit. This isn't a casual project but a struggle for the very nature of the future. We understand that most won't be interested or lack the discipline necessary for our grand duty." She gestured around the room. "Note how none of the others returned. We're used to that. Even magicals with the potential for long lifespans still think like short-lived and short-sighted beings." She looked from student to student until her gaze stopped on Madelyn.

The friends let that sink in and no one spoke.

"This might be something you want to spend time thinking about," Cina said. "It'll enable you to fully digest what I've said to you. I thank you all for coming, and I would suggest you spend a couple of weeks in reflection before we talk again."

Philip stood first and his bored expression made it clear he wanted to leave as soon as possible. Raine almost laughed when she realized she'd effectively ruined a Saturday not only for her and Cameron but also for all her friends. She wasn't fully convinced it had been the best use of her time but also wasn't sure if Cina had some kind of scam in mind or if she was merely delusional. There was zero evidence the Thothites had access to unusual magic, and the woman's explanations weren't convincing. The evidence pointed more toward cult than con artists.

The other students stood and Madelyn rose last.

They were almost to the hallway when the priestess called, "Madelyn, might I speak with you for a moment alone?"

The girl blinked and turned. "Excuse me?"

Cina smiled at her. "Everyone else spoke and asked questions, but you didn't. Perhaps things would be more comfortable if we spoke alone. That way, you wouldn't worry about being embarrassed in front of your friends."

Madelyn took a deep breath and shook her head. "It's not that I'm embarrassed."

The woman advanced on her, an almost hungry look in

her eye. "Sometimes, we can feel anxiety and not even understand the source. I think you would feel more comfortable if we could speak alone, if only for a moment."

"I-I'm not comfortable with that," the elf stammered. Her desperate gaze cut toward the others. "I'd like my friends to be here."

Raine frowned. "If Madelyn's not comfortable staying by herself, she doesn't have to."

Cina took another step. "Don't you think that's presumptuous? Maybe she's only afraid to talk because you've not let her think for herself."

Cameron and Adrien advanced to stand on either side of Madelyn, their expressions tight.

"I don't think that's the case." Raine stepped in front of her.

The woman's mouth twitched with what might have been irritation. "Don't be so small-minded."

"Excuse me?"

Cina pointed at the elf, a deep frown on her face. "You need to give her the chance to grow. That can happen with the Children of Thoth."

Madelyn took a deep breath. "I want to go now."

Raine nodded. "Yes, I think we should go."

"You can't stand in the way of the future," Cina shouted. "Do you want to start standing in the way now? If you do, you're no better than those who oppressed us in the past."

"Let's get out of here." Raine put her hand on Madelyn's back.

Cina stepped forward, only to be met by Cameron. He uttered a small growl and his eyes flashed yellow.

"Don't," the shifter muttered warningly. "Just don't."

Adrien raised a hand but didn't summon a sword. Evie's hand drifted to a pouch on her belt and Sara drew a small acorn from her pocket. William raised his palm with a frown and his eyes flashed with flames. Philip pulled his wand out. Raine stood in front of Madelyn, her hands on her hips as she glared at the Thothite priestess.

Cina stepped back and shook her head. A smile returned but it didn't reach her eyes. "I'm sorry. I've perhaps been too enthusiastic, and I see you have misinterpreted it. I meant no harm and hope you all come to our next meeting. I think you'll find you won't have a greater opportunity to have a more positive influence on the future than with the Children of Thoth."

The students edged toward the hallway. Everyone surrounded Madelyn and watched Cina with suspicion. The formation didn't break up until they stepped out of the hallway, through the double doors, and onto the street. The woman made no further attempt to follow them.

Raine looked at her hand. At some point during their escape, Madelyn had grabbed it.

"Are you okay?" she asked.

The girl nodded. "The way she looked at me scared me."

Adrien frowned. "Yes. What was that about? Why was she so obsessed with talking to Madelyn alone?"

Cameron stared at the wide blue building and growled. "Something else is going on here. This isn't simply about a scheme or multi-level marketing. We can't play around with this anymore. We need to talk to someone."

Raine nodded. "I don't know what the Thothites are up to, but it probably wouldn't hurt to tell someone to take a closer look at them." She squeezed Madelyn's hand. "Let's get you back to school for now."

"There might be a problem with that," Adrien said. He raised his hand and summoned a sword.

Eight men rushed down the street, all with wands in their hands. She recognized at least three of them from the previous week's meeting. Apparently, Cina wasn't willing to wait.

CHAPTER TWENTY-NINE

Raine yanked her wand out and spun toward the double doors to cast a hurried locking spell. It wouldn't hold any serious attempt to breach it, but she hoped it would at least stop anyone else from easily surprising them.

The students' experience showed in their immediate responses. Everyone layered a shield over themselves. Cameron shifted and uttered a loud, long growl. Adrien immediately began to chant a spell, his gaze fixed on the men in front of them.

The Thothites slowed, deep frowns on their faces.

One of them glared at Cameron. "Put your wands down and your hands on your heads. Have the wolf shift back to human forms. We don't want to hurt you kids, but we can't let you cause trouble. You have to walk away from this and go home." He nodded toward Madelyn. "Leave the Coral Elf."

Raine looked around. The street was empty other than the students and the Thothites. Someone would hear the sounds of a battle, but there would be no one to back them up, and that was assuming anyone else would dare to get involved. "She called them here."

The doors to the building burst open and made a mockery of Raine's locking spell. Cina marched out, her scowl one of disapproval and irritation. Magic radiated off her, but her wand remained undrawn.

"I'm sorry to have to do this," she said. "But I can't take any risks now that I'm so close. You should have simply let me talk to her."

"Let us go," Raine demanded. "This doesn't have to end badly. I don't know what this is about, but you haven't done anything yet. You can still walk away."

Her companions remained alert but some kept their attention on the eight men. Philip, Evie, and Raine focused on the priestess, their wands ready.

Cina shook her head. "Take the Coral Elf," she shouted to her men. "Avoid hurting the others too badly if you can but do what you must."

"You won't take Madelyn," Raine shouted.

The girl blinked and jerked her head in panic, her eyes wide. "Why me?"

Adrien finished his chant. Four illusionary fakes winked into existence. The five copies moved toward the Thothites who hesitated, unprepared for the rapid defense. Apparently, Louper teams were more prepared to deal with his trick than their current adversaries. Maybe kidnapping wasn't a common activity for them.

Cameron loped after the group of replicas and howled. Perhaps the authorities would respond faster if they thought a shifter was out of control.

Sara arced a berry toward the Thothites a moment later. It exploded in a blinding shower of sparks. The enemy stumbled back amidst groans and some threw their arms over their eyes. William blasted a yellow-red orb directly toward them that exploded in another blinding flare.

Adrien burst over the blinded group of men, his sword in hand. He landed and spun with his blade raised to chant another quick spell. A crescent of white-blue light erupted from the blade and struck one of the wizards, who collapsed with a low moan. The seven remaining men split their attention between the elf behind them and the other students.

Raine ignored the front group and shouted a restraint spell. She conjured a thin rope that streaked toward Cina but the priestess made no attempt to draw her wand. Instead, she flicked her wrist. A pulse of magic thrummed from her before flames consumed the rope and it turned into ash. Evie lobbed a potion at her. The priestess made another quick movement with her hand and thrust the potion aside. It shattered on the ground and a web of strands grew from the sizzling liquid.

Philip tried a more straight-forward stun spell and managed to release a weak white-blue bolt at the woman. The energy spread against her shield but she didn't twitch or cry out.

Cina thrust her hand forward. A wave of force struck the students and they catapulted and tumbled as if back-handed by a rabid Kilomea. A thick, acrid mist erupted above Raine and drifted over her. She began to cough and tears streamed from her eyes. Despite her discomfort, she scrabbled around her, located her wand, and managed to stutter an incantation.

A bubble of clean air formed around her head and pushed the smothering mist away. Another spasm of coughs overtook her.

She stood, her limbs trembling and her wand pointed, but she couldn't make anything out except shadows. After another breath of clean air, she waved her wand and murmured an air stream spell. The mists began to flow away to reveal Evie, then Sara, both with reddened eyes and air bubbles now protecting them. A moment later, she saw everyone else, including four of the Thothites on the ground, bound in thick rope and their wands several yards away.

Adrien stood near them with a frown, his sword pointed down. Cameron sprinted toward her and shifted into human form a yard away.

He coughed a few times and wiped his mouth on his sleeve. "Adrien got a bubble around me, but not before I sucked in a few breaths of that. Are you okay?"

Raine nodded and studied their surroundings quickly. Cina was gone, and she didn't see any of the other Thothites. Her stomach lurched, and she spun to search the area frantically. It hadn't been that long, but there were many, many ways to move quickly when magic was involved.

"Madelyn!" she shouted. "Where are you?"

Sara and Evie gasped and began their own hurried scan. Cameron and William started searching, concern on their faces. Philip cursed.

"We need to get the kemana police," Adrien shouted.

"Cina must have her, and I don't know what this is about, but if she's gone to all this trouble, it can't be good."

"We don't have time." Raine shook her head. "I'm beginning to think Cina wasn't lying about having special power. She cast spells without her wand, incantations, or even much movement."

"It's not the time to be impressed," Cameron pointed out and growled his anger. "We need to find Madelyn." He shifted into wolf form and sniffed the ground for a moment before a low rumble issued from his throat and he pointed his nose into the distance.

"Do you have a scent?" Raine asked.

The wolf bobbed his head.

"He's right," she said. "We need to go. We don't have time to wait for the police."

"What about those four?" William asked and pointed to the Thothites.

"I'll handle it," Adrien said. He placed his hand on top of one of the restrained men and murmured a spell. The man jerked before he fell unconscious. The elf repeated the process with the other three.

Cameron padded down the road and sniffed intermittently along the ground. The others jogged after him. A block later, they caught sight of four men racing along with a robed woman in white. Madelyn floated through the air behind Cina, her eyes closed.

The students surged forward. The fugitives turned to launch fireballs, no longer interested in minimizing casualties.

The Trouble Squad scattered as the deadly magical blasts careened past or exploded nearby. Sara hurled another berry toward them but when it exploded this time, the men's eyes glowed and they showed no sign of being blinded. Philip's quick slime spell coated an invisible shield that extended a yard from his target.

"Give her back," Raine shouted. If they raised enough of a ruckus, someone else had to come.

Cina continued to jog down the street without even a glance at her pursuers. Madelyn continued to drift behind her.

Raine gritted her teeth. With the change in the running battle from stuns and rope to fireballs, the police would come eventually, but the kemana authorities always seemed slow to respond. Her experience with the druids when she'd first arrived and other subsequent incidents had already convinced her that her knowledge of when and how the authorities responded to trouble had been hopelessly wrong. It hadn't taken long to realize that her experiences growing up in a non-magical city didn't prepare her for the less efficient response in a place like Ruby Falls. It might not be the Wild West, but it got closer to that than she liked at times.

William held both palms up. A stream of tiny flaming spheres burst from his palms and arced toward the men. Their shields absorbed the blows but distracted the targets.

"Go, Raine," Adrien shouted. "We'll hold them here."

Raine pointed her wand down and shouted a burst spell. While she had never been as good at the technique as Adrien, she still had some proficiency. She'd come a long way from the ignorant new witch of her freshman year, and she would demonstrate that to anyone who wanted to hurt her friends.

The motion carried her up and over until she landed on the angled roof of a nearby building. A few people stared at her from one street over, hopefully more witnesses to summon the police. Another couple of bursts almost brought her to her quarry. Cameron rushed past the men, but he was well behind Raine and Cina and a few fireballs forced him to take cover.

The priestess shook her head and sighed. She produced a tiny glass bead from under her belt and threw it in front of her. Smoke poured out and coalesced into a portal that revealed the front of a tall white building. She stepped through and Madelyn floated after her.

Raine gasped. She launched off the side of the building and cast another burst spell that rocketed her toward the portal. It began to shrink as she approached. Ten feet. Five feet. Three feet.

The portal collapsed scant seconds after Raine passed through it and she sprawled painfully onto cobblestones. Pain radiated through her shoulder but her shield saved her from serious injury.

Cina stopped and turned, her eyes narrowed. Madelyn floated gently to the ground.

Raine looked up and immediately recognized the building. They were still in the kemana and not halfway around the world. She could still save her friend.

The priestess clucked her tongue impatiently. "You're quite persistent, aren't you?"

CHAPTER THIRTY

It took determination, but Raine forced herself to her feet and pointed her wand at Cina. She drew a few deep breaths. "Give my friend back. I don't care about any of your big plans. All I want is Madelyn."

Several tall windowless buildings stood in the area, intercut with small alleys. Only the one main street ran in front of them. She had been in this part of Ruby Falls a few times while exploring, but it hadn't been for a while. There weren't any stores in the area, mostly warehouses from what she understood.

The woman shook her head. "You have to believe me when I say I really don't want to hurt you, Raine. You're persistent, intelligent, loyal, and brave. In any other circumstance, I would try to recruit you as a member of the Children of Thoth. Everything I've told you is the truth. Our goals are noble and will help the future."

"You forgot to mention the part about being kidnappers in your sales pitch." She narrowed her eyes. "It makes it hard to believe you're really so noble. Maybe you weren't so oppressed in the past."

Cina shook her head and the familiar soft smile returned. "We were, though. Do you really buy into all the lies they've told you? It's not too late, Raine. You can be part of a future that isn't dependent on gates, a future where Earth isn't constrained by something that can't even be controlled. It's capricious and cruel."

She flung her hand in the air and pointed toward the glowing roof of the kemana. "A future where people don't have to depend on hiding their power in periods of darkness. Think about all the people who have died on Earth in the last few thousands of years who could have been saved by healing magic. Think of the tyrants who could have been stopped with magic." She shook her head. "If we had full access to magic, Earth could have been a paradise, not a war-wracked planet that has taken millennia to grow toward anything approaching true balance. The Children of Thoth can unlock that power."

Raine held her wand at the ready. "Oriceran isn't paradise. They had the Great War. Maybe if we had magic, we would have had something as awful as that."

"Yes, they had their Great War. But think about it. They had it and then they had three thousand years of peace. A few skirmishes here and there isn't the same as a war." Cina uttered a harsh laugh. "We had our own Great War and a few decades later, we had a worse war with even worse weapons. Don't you see? Technology's a dead-end, a false tool that dulls the spirit. Magic will lead Earth to greatness and peace, but only if we can free it from the dependence on Oriceran and the gates. Some sacrifices will have to be made along the way for that goal, but it's necessary."

"I don't understand what Madelyn has to do with any of this." Her gaze darted to the girl, who was unconscious but breathing.

The lack of nearby smoke or sounds of battle suggested Raine's friends were fighting the other Thothites a fair distance away. Although she faced one-on-one odds, the abilities Cina had already demonstrated suggested she might not be able to defeat the witch alone—if that's what the priestess was. She cast spells without a wand, which at least raised some doubts. Still, Raine didn't understand why she would lie about being a witch.

Had Cina truly unlocked some great power beyond normal magic?

"Madelyn's a key," the woman said. "I know you can't understand that and I wish I had time to teach it to you. Maybe this was a mistake, but you don't understand. We've waited for over a thousand years." She gestured toward the Coral Elf. "We waited for the Twin Keys of Maat. Some gave up along the way, forgot what we were doing, and doubted we would find them. Then they simply wandered into this place. Prophecy is always easy to doubt until it becomes reality."

"Prophecy?" Raine narrowed her eyes. "That's what you think this is about?"

"It's what I know this is about."

Madelyn's eyes flickered open, and she blinked several times. Raine shook her head slightly, hoping her adversary wouldn't understand she was trying to communicate with her friend.

"You don't believe me?" the priestess asked. "Of course you don't. You're only a child." She sighed and took a deep breath. "Don't make me kill you, Raine. You were born on Earth. You have to understand what I'm doing is for this planet's benefit. For humanity's benefit. I'm not a wicked witch planning to wage war on Oriceran. This ends in peace and plenty, not more blood."

"Diseased trees grow from bad seeds," she replied.

Cina looked confused. "Meaning what?"

"I have one question for you. I won't bother with a truth spell, but I have a good idea I'll know if you're lying. Your response to the question will determine if I walk away."

"Very well. Ask your question."

She swallowed. "You don't even have to explain what you plan to do to Madelyn. All I want to know is if she'll be okay afterward."

The woman pursed her lips. "She'll help usher in a new age."

"That's not what I asked. Do you intend to hurt her?"

"Some keys get stuck in their locks." She sighed. "If there was any other way, I would take it, but what little possibilities we had are gone. You made that clear."

Raine slapped her free hand on her chest and kept her wand pointed at Cina. "What? How is this my fault?"

"I'm not saying it's your fault, but you said her sister was dead. Is that true?"

Madelyn remained prone, but the pain was obvious in her eyes.

"Yes, Vianna died last spring." She nodded at the Coral Elf. "For her sister's sake. Vianna was a brave girl who knew her sister would grow stronger eventually, and even if she were scared, she could get by with the help of friends like me." She pointed her wand toward the sky and hoped fervently that the other girl would take the hint as she prepared for her next move. "And I swore to help her, so I intend to do that now."

Cina stared at her wand. "You intend to give up?"

Raine made a few quick movements and uttered an incantation. A bright red-and-white ball of flame erupted from the tip of her wand and traveled into the sky where it exploded in a shower of sparks that spelled, *HELP ME! KIDNAPPER!*

The priestess shook her head, her expression tight and guarded. "You could flee from me, but you can't defeat me and take your friend with you."

"I don't need to win against you." She lowered her wand until it pointed at her adversary again. "That doesn't mean I can't annoy you a little."

"Go ahead. Attack me. Understand the futility of what you do. You can't win against me."

She pointed her wand at Cina's leg before she locked gazes with Madelyn. "You don't have to do this either." She shouted the fireball incantation.

A bright ball of flame screamed toward her quarry and exploded. The smoke and flame died down to reveal that the attack hadn't pierced her defenses. Her white robe remained pristine and her eyes were filled with pity.

"All your friends together might have a small chance against me." The priestess raised her hand. "But alone?" She cut through the air with her hand.

Pain exploded through Raine's side as she catapulted

back, but she kept her wand pointed at Cina. She managed to release an ice lance before she landed hard and rolled. The attack bounced off the other witch and the projectile shattered harmlessly against the ground.

Madelyn stood, her eyes wide and her knees shaking. Cina's attention remained focused on her attacker and not the girl who now stood behind her.

Raine pushed to her feet and wiped blood off her mouth. She summoned a new shield. "If you already have access to primordial magic, why do you need Madelyn? Something doesn't seem right about this."

Cina narrowed her eyes. "Bravery is noble, Raine, but throwing your life away is pointless."

"Defending your friends is never pointless."

She aimed her wand at the witch's head. This time, instead of a fireball, she cast a blinding spell. A kaleidoscopic ball streaked out and exploded in a shower of multi-colored sparks. The Thothite sighed and shook her head.

Madelyn took the opportunity to run. Raine launched another blinding spell followed by a couple of fireballs. Her opponent simply stood in silence with a disappointed look on her face as the spells struck her.

"Are you finished with this tantrum?" Cina asked finally.

Raine waited with a grin until the Coral Elf disappeared into the narrow space between two of the nearby buildings.

"It's also not pointless to distract someone while your friend escapes," she said.

The woman's eyes widened and she spun to see for

herself. "Impossible." She sighed. "I'll track her. You've only delayed the inevitable."

"Then I'll keep you busy. You said it before. I'm very persistent."

Cina flicked a finger and a crackling bolt of energy struck Raine. She blinked to regain her focus, and it took her several seconds to realize she'd been hurled several yards away from her original position. For a moment, she lay flat on her back, her muscles sore and twitching.

Her hand also twitched, but her fingers clung to her wand. She grimaced and staggered to her feet, her shirt charred, and her body throbbed with pain. Loud shouts resounded nearby. Wizards bounded over the rooftops and raced through the streets.

"Can you take on the Ruby Falls police, too?" Raine managed to ask, her voice hoarse. "I already know you can't portal simply anywhere. So much for all your power."

"You understand nothing." The priestess shook her head, her face twisted in shock and disbelief. "And you have no idea what you've done."

"I know exactly what I've done. I've saved my friend."

Cina retrieved another bead from her belt. "The Coral Elf is the only Key of Maat left. This doesn't end here. It only postpones things." She threw the pebble and stepped through the portal. It winked out of existence a moment later.

Raine fell to her hands and knees and her entire body ached. She had no doubt her adversary could have killed her if she had wanted to, but it didn't matter as long as she saved Madelyn.

The girl poked her head out of the small alley and

rushed over to her. Tears ran down her cheeks "A-are you okay?"

"I've been better, and Cameron will be angry." She lay down and rolled onto her back. "How about you?"

Madelyn knelt in front of her and placed her friend's head in her lap. "I'm fine." She shook her head. "No, I'm not. I thought I was so brave after everything with Erin, but I was useless. I froze during the first fight, and then I sat and cowered. I'm still useless." She sniffled as more tears welled. "Vianna died because I'm worthless, and you were hurt because I'm worthless."

Raine stroked her cheek tenderly. "You're not worthless. Not immediately being good in a fight doesn't mean anything. The fact that I have so much experience simply means I get in too much trouble." She laughed quietly. "You did fine. And sometimes, the best thing you can do is run away." She winced. "You can't win every fight, but the important thing is that sometimes, you don't have to win the fight to win the situation."

The loud thuds of boots announced the arrival of the Ruby Falls police.

"What's going on here?" a policeman shouted and swept the area with his wand at the ready.

"We have a little something to report about the Children of Thoth," she muttered.

CHAPTER THIRTY-ONE

Raine couldn't look Headmistress Berens in the eye and instead, focused on the woman's desk. The deep frown on her face intimidated her. The headmistress had already discussed the situation with everyone else and had saved her for last. Agent Connor stood off to the side, his arms folded. His expression didn't scream pleased either. She hadn't held back any detail as she related everything that had led to her confrontation with Cina.

"Let me be clear, Raine," the headmistress said. "I'm proud of you and your friends, but I'm also disappointed."

She looked up, a little startled. "What? I don't understand."

The woman looked at Agent Connor and nodded.

He stepped forward and lowered his arms. "Evidence leads the case."

"But instincts lead you to evidence," she intoned. She sighed. "My instincts were right. There was something weird about the Thothites."

He shook his head. "Let's make this a teachable

moment. I want you to explain to me and the headmistress where exactly you went wrong. You weren't incorrect in saying that sending the authorities after the Thothites with no evidence of wrongdoing wasn't appropriate. That said, there is a clear moment of failure here where you exceeded the risk you should take as a student and didn't make use of the appropriate resources. That choice led to unnecessary danger for you and your friends, and although we're proud of how you defended Madelyn, we wish you hadn't ended up in that position, to begin with."

Raine took a deep breath and thought over the last couple of weeks. "It went wrong when I decided to take Madelyn to the second meeting without informing you and the headmistress. I already had some suspicion of Cina, so at that point, at the minimum, I should have talked to you and voiced my suspicions. Even if I ended up going there to see what was going on, I could have had additional people to protect me."

"Exactly. Infiltration of groups is always a difficult and dangerous job, and information exchanged with others is critical for its success." Agent Connor frowned, his face set in a stern expression. "Which is why it's so important to make sure everyone knows what's going on. Whether or not we would have allowed you to do that is a separate question, but the important thing is you should plan for situations like that to go badly." He looked at the headmistress.

She nodded and her frown eased. "But we won't complain about how you and the others tried to prevent the kidnapping. Based on the short-range portal beads Cina used, if it weren't for your immediate actions, she might very well have escaped with Madelyn, and it's obvious that her plans for the girl wouldn't end well."

Raine sighed. "I still don't understand what is going on and why they wanted her. Or the power she showed. Maybe she was telling the truth."

Headmistress Berens scoffed. "She might very well believe that nonsense, but I suspect the artifact pendant she wears can be used as a natural channel of her power, which eliminates her need for a wand. If the Thothites had access to special magic, why did any of her underlings bother with normal wands? And why did she need artifacts to portal?"

"I didn't think of that."

"Exactly." The woman sighed. "Unfortunately, the Ruby Falls authorities weren't able to get much out of the captured underlings. Mostly, they have admitted to the same things Cina already told you concerning a prophecy leading to ancient power. They all genuinely seem to believe in it."

"The Twin Keys of Maat," Raine intoned. "But what was the prophecy?"

The headmistress frowned. "None of them know the exact prophecy or the source. Apparently, only Cina knew. She said it involved two blue-haired sisters who were of this world but not of it, but those are the only details she shared with her followers."

She gasped. "I have to admit that sounds a lot like Vianna and Madelyn."

Agent Connor snorted. "Just because magic's real doesn't mean prophecies can't be made to fit a lot of different situations. The ability to cast spells doesn't mean you can't be deluded."

"I can't speak to the accuracy of the prophecy, especially since I don't know the whole thing," the woman began, "but the underlings have admitted they've been here far longer than Cina implied to you, and that she told them she had sensed something unusual in this area."

"But she didn't know Vianna was dead," Raine pointed out.

"There are still many questions that remain regarding the incident. What we do know is that they lived in the kemana for some time based on this potentially dubious prophecy." She frowned. "And it's obvious their targets from the beginning were Vianna and Madelyn. She might even have had some magical method that determined you had a connection to her, which explains why she approached you instead of other students."

Agent Connor grunted. "Not only that, but it's obvious she spent some time profiling you as a target."

"What do you mean?"

"I contacted OAAS," Headmistress Berens said. "They have no record of a student matching her description and name. Your involvement in the project over the summer is hardly secret, and although we've taken efforts to keep you from being harassed by curious people, the discoveries on that island are of such importance that it's inevitable dubious people learned of it and your involvement along with the others. That probably explains why she claimed to be an alumnus."

Raine frowned. "You're saying it was a set-up from the beginning?"

The agent nodded. "Most likely. From what the headmistress has explained to me, it might have initially required magic to determine the connections, and Cina refined it. She probably combined it with other more conventional investigation techniques. I've contacted the FBI and Agent Oliver for preliminary information on the Children of Thoth, and they both told me the same thing, which matches with what Cina told you. The group was all but dead for a thousand years until the gates began to open. They've been investigated in the recent past by the FBI and PDA, but until this latest incident, they've never been found to have done anything illegal."

Headmistress Berens folded her hands in front of her. "I would like you to avoid the kemana, at least for a little while, but as we're going into the end of the semester, you'll be busy anyway.

"What about Madelyn?"

"We'll keep her on campus until she's safe. Cina escaped, and everything she said to you suggests she's not about to give up on the girl. No one wants any of the good progress Madelyn's made disrupted by attacks, let alone for her to get hurt." She frowned. "She is a student of this school, and we'll protect her until such time as the woman is apprehended."

Raine nodded. "I hope she's caught soon."

"I'm sure everyone does."

Madelyn twirled on skates atop another Dorvu-sourced ice rink. The temperatures had dipped enough that the ice might last a few days without magical aid. Raine had purchased her proper ice skates in the hope that a hobby not totally dependent on magic might further engage her in the world.

"I'm fine with not visiting the kemana," the elf declared when she stopped her twirl. "I don't like going there much anyway, and Erin's not allowed to go yet. I have the most fun with you and the others on movie night."

Raine nodded. She'd sought the girl out shortly after finishing with the headmistress and Agent Connor. "They'll catch Cina. She's a criminal now, but until then, you'll be safe here."

"I know." She gave a soft smile. "I was scared when I saw you hurt, but afterward, I...it's weird." She sighed.

"What?"

"It made me happy." She skated toward the other end before she swept around the rink toward Raine. "I feel like you and the others actually care about me. Erin does, too. I never knew anyone except my sister could truly care about me, but this semester has changed all that. I'll miss you all during the break, but I have plenty of skating and reading to do to keep me busy until you get back."

"And you're not worried about Cina? It's okay if you are."

Madelyn shook her head. "I'm patient. I don't know why she thinks me and Vianna are important to her prophecy, but it doesn't matter as long as I'm at the School of Necessary Magic and have friends and professors who care about me. I finally realized and accepted something you had all told me."

"Which is what exactly?" Raine asked.

"I am real. Not because I have a body. Not because of magic or anything. I'm real because I care about others and others care about me." The girl turned a few times, her arms out. "I have a new family here at the School of Necessary Magic."

"That you do, Madelyn. That you do, and we'll do everything we can to keep you safe and help you have a good time."

CHAPTER THIRTY-TWO

"Raine, wait," Head Librarian Decker called to her as she left the library for the last time that semester.

She turned with a smile. "Don't worry. I've returned everything I borrowed. Even that ancient maps book I've been so obsessed with."

The gnome chuckled. "I'm glad to hear that, but it's not what I'm concerned about." His expression grew serious. "I've always strived to help you and lead you on the right path, and I realized that I might have made a mistake this semester, and so I needed to acknowledge that now."

"What are you talking about? What mistake?" she asked, genuinely confused

"The Children of Thoth." He shook his head regretfully. "I suggested to you that they weren't dangerous, and that mistake could have been deadly to you and any of your friends. So I wanted to apologize. I fed you misleading information, and that's one of the worst things a librarian can do."

Raine shook her head. "I can't accept your apology."

His face paled a little with surprise. "Very well. I'm disappointed, but I respect your position."

"No, you don't understand. I can't accept your apology because you did nothing wrong. Giving me knowledge to the best of your ability is all I can ask from you. You're a gnome, not a Seer, and without your help throughout my time here, I don't know where I would be." She grinned. "And let's be honest. We both know I get in trouble because I can't help but stick my nose into business that I probably shouldn't. I'm not sure I would have done things differently if you had told me the Children used to be dangerous."

Head Librarian Decker nodded slowly. "I care about you, Raine. You're one of my favorite students in a long time. I know I'll worry about you joining the FBI, and there is only so much I can do to help or guide an FBI agent. But know that while you're still here, I'll do everything I can to help you."

"I know that, and you already have." Raine turned and her gaze traversed the rows of books, ladders, desks, tables, and chairs. "This place is special to me, and I'll remember it long after I graduate. You helped me find my place in this temple of learning, and I'll be forever grateful. I'll be a better FBI agent because I had access to a great library and a great librarian."

He chuckled. "An odd and rare sentiment, I'm sure. These books will wait for your return as eagerly as I will."

She waved cheerfully. "I'm glad I spent more time here this semester. I'll see you soon."

Raine moved to Evie, Sara, and Madelyn, in turn, to hug them tightly. She had stood on the edge of the circle drive with her suitcase, waiting for the jitney to take her to Starbucks.

With the end of the semester, it was time for everyone to return home, but she left a little earlier than any of her other friends because Uncle Jerry wanted her home for a little party. He wanted to show off his little future FBI witch to some old agency friends in town. She considered it part of helping to draw magicals and non-magicals together, and it never hurt to soak in a little more wisdom from former agents.

"We've gone through this so many times," she murmured, "but it never gets any easier. I hate this part."

Sara gave her a playful grin. "I know what you mean, but we'd probably get sick of each other if we saw each other all the time." She leaned forward and winked. "Keep in mind that applies to boyfriends as well."

"I mentioned how much your uncle lets Cameron stay with you to my family." Evie blushed. "I'm trying to convince them to let William stay over, if not now, then at least after graduation for a while. I know he likes staying with the pack, but it wouldn't hurt to spend a little time away from the school with me."

"We're grabbing more boyfriend time and exposing them to the families?" Sara tilted her head in thought. "I don't know if Philip is ready for my family. They would eat him alive. I love them, but kitsune families aren't for the faint of heart."

Raine smiled at Madelyn. "I wish you could spend your break with me. Stupid Cina. If she hadn't tried her garbage,

I'm sure they wouldn't have restricted you to campus. You were so close to getting permission to go places besides the kemana."

The elf shook her head. "Even if it wasn't for Cina, I don't think the PDA would be comfortable with that. I'm sure by the time I graduate, I'll be ready for normal cities, but I'm fine now. Thanks to all of you. Thank you for everything—not only the Thothites but caring from the beginning, and for movie night and not making fun of me because of the first movie I brought." She wiped a happy tear away. "I might have lost my sister, but I feel like I have three new big sisters. This school is beginning to feel like home to me."

Evie teared up and turned away. "You're welcome, Madelyn."

Sara dabbed at her eyes. "Damn mold allergies," she joked. "I need to develop the ultimate anti-histamine spell."

Raine gave Madelyn another hug. "We'll be here for you next semester, and we'll visit after that. And you have Erin, too."

Someone cleared his throat from behind them. Raine pulled away from the hug to find Cameron, William, Philip, and Adrien behind her.

The shifter frowned. "Did you plan to take off without saying goodbye?" He nodded to the suitcase and raised an eyebrow.

Her cheeks heated. They'd already shared a rather passionate goodbye kiss about a half-hour before, and she'd thought that was goodbye. She didn't realize he was joking until he grinned.

"Don't mess with me like that," she whined.

He scoffed and rolled his eyes. "I still owe you ten years of being messed with given some of the stuff you put me through. But I'll put up with it since I love you."

Philip made a gagging sound. "Get a room, you two."

Sara glared at him. "You object to love?"

The wizard winced. "No, no." He waved his hands. "I love you, too, you know." He blushed and looked down.

Evie and William didn't say anything but he took her hand in his.

Adrien smiled. "This has been a good semester. It would have been better with Christie, but we upheld justice and the Cardinals are still undefeated. There's little more I could ask for out of my time here. It's always invigorating."

The half-Ifrit turned to Madelyn. "We still haven't taken you to a Louper match. You're a lot more comfortable with people now. You really should consider it."

She shrugged. "It's...too much. Sorry." She looked apologetically at Adrien. "I'm sure you and the others are wonderful, but I don't want to be around so many people. I'm even a little nervous right now with all these other people besides you around, but I wanted to make sure I saw Raine off."

"It's fine. I'm not offended." The Light Elf shrugged. "Some people don't even like Louper, but I would play even if there were no fans. It's nice to have supporters, but my drive comes from within and not from without."

William sighed.

Adrien looked over at him with concern. "What's wrong?"

"I'm really feeling it now with all of us standing out here." He gestured at several other students who chatted nearby with their luggage beside them. "It's the end of our first semester of our final year. We're graduating in less than half a year. It was just…" He shook his head. "It's hard to think about. It makes me think about freshmen year and then I get all nostalgic and…I don't know, I feel weird."

Sara grinned. "Tick-tock, the clock always moves, old man, and you can't escape its touch. Will you go to the freshmen and give them a big speech about, 'Back in my day, we snuck into the kemana with one person doing the stealth spell, and we liked it, but you kids are all spoiled?'"

They all laughed, even Madelyn.

The half-Ifrit raised a hand and a small flame appeared. "I accepted who and what I am at this school with the help of all of you."

Philip groaned. "Don't get us all weepy, dude. Let's keep it breezy. I was half-convinced the Cardinals going undefeated for the first half of the season would be the most exciting thing that happened this semester, but I should have known better."

Cameron put his arm around Raine. "I've given up on having a quiet semester. I think I'd be kind of freaked out if we actually had one, so I'll settle for any semester where we learn something and help someone out. We're leaving the world a better place each time, and that's not so bad."

Raine leaned into her boyfriend. "I'll settle for any semester I get to spend with the people I care about. I'll miss you all when I graduate, but we still have a final semester. So let's make it great."

Adrien nodded. "I will deliver the championship. I can promise that."

Philip stuck his hand out, palm down. They all eyed him.

"Problem?" Adrien asked.

"No. No problem. The mood struck me." He smiled sheepishly. "And I wanted to do an FBI Trouble Squad cheer. Okay, it's dumb. I'm sorry."

Raine grinned and pulled away from Cameron. She stuck her hand on top of his. "It's not dumb. It sounds fun, and we might as well have fun while we're still in school."

The shifter chuckled and added his hand. Evie, William, and Adrien all added theirs.

"Come on, Madelyn. You, too." Raine nodded to their hands.

The Coral Elf eyed the others with unease. "But I'm not a member of the FBI Trouble Squad. I'm more of a source of trouble for you all. I'm not even a senior."

"You're an honorary member." She nodded toward their hands. "And you risked yourself on a Trouble Squad case." She shook her head. "No, that's wrong. You're not an honorary member. You're a full member. Get in here already and stop trying to convince yourself you're not one of us."

The others shouted their encouragement. Madelyn hesitated for a few more seconds before she placed her hand on the top.

"FBI Trouble Squad!"

The story is far from over. Raine's high school adventures conclude in A NECESSARY WITCH

FREE BOOKS!

For Hire: Teachers for special school in Virginia countryside.

Must be able to handle teenagers with special abilities.

Cannot be afraid to discipline werewolves, wizards, elves and other assorted hormonal teens.

Apply at the School of Necessary Magic.

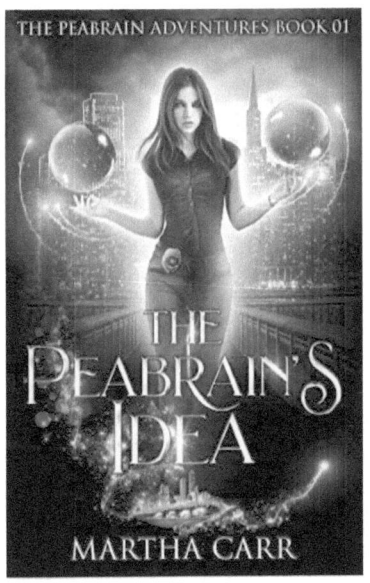

**Find the compass, save the world or
save herself?**

Dating is harder for Maggie Parker than running down a felon. Now add in magic.

Did she just see a compass fly?

Can she learn how to use the magic of bubbles to chart a new course in time? It's a lot harder than it sounds.

Join her on her quest to rescue passengers on an ancient ship – a big blue marble called Earth – and save herself.

AVAILABLE ON AMAZON AND IN KINDLE UNLIMITED!

Fun fact – Cowboy boots were first invented to stave off snake bites in Texas. That old nugget has popped back into my brain because lately, my small neighborhood has become rattler central.

We've had so many four and five-foot rattlesnakes show up in backyards that we made the local news. It's rarely good when you look up and recognize the houses and realize, that's your house. There have been so many snakes that a neighbor with a snake grabber and the right kind of courage has gotten a little side business going. She takes tips…

There have been so many snakes that there's a snake meeting planned to talk about it. I have a stronger feeling about meetings than I do about snakes and may not attend. Meetings with Craig Martelle or Michael Anderle tend to be fun and there's generally food, but besides those two as hosts, it's hard to get me to accept.

The pictures have been flying on Facebook of different coiled snakes, but my favorite picture so far has been the one that shows a very large snake coiled in the air, head bent forward, rattler shaking. It was dark and my neighbor thought the sprinklers were going off till she shined her phone light on it.

My friends Nicole and Steve right up the street heard about the snakes in the area when they first moved in and put snake fencing all around their backyard. They have cats and two St. Bernard's and wanted to be sure. You can see this one coming, right? Steve was outside on the porch with some boxes and the cat. He kicked a box and heard a rattle. He grabbed the cat and ran inside, after grabbing photographic proof. It was a big one.

Turns out there was one small hole in all that fencing, and the snake found it. I think the rattler took it as a challenge, which is just like anything from Texas.

I grew up running through woods a lot of my childhood and was warned about rattlesnakes and cotton mouths. I seem to recall being told that you can't even outrun a snake. They can move faster. That may be fake news pre-internet days so check that one before you share it. But what I learned that is actually true and useful was to have a healthy respect without living in fear. That's a necessary combo in order to build a bigger life.

Otherwise, if I chose trying to protect against what *might* happen, I wouldn't drive my Subaru on those hairy overpasses here that have no sides to them so you can see where your car can go over while taking that sharp curve in the sky. (Okay, subtext – I'm from Chicago where everything is flat – no overpasses, not even a nice hill - and it feels like Texas has set up a sneaky kind of thrill ride every time I'm headed downtown.)

Instead, I know what to do just in case and take reasonable precautions. This past week I've been walking the property ahead of the good dog Lois Lane and the sweet pittie, Leela looking for snakes and so far, no visitors. Both of those dogs would chase a snake and they might win, but I'd prefer not to find out. Upside is I've gotten to see the stars out at night and a few sunrises and sunsets. Love a big Texas sky.

I haven't invested in cowboy boots yet, which is surprising considering that it's like owning slippers in these parts. It's just something you do. I suppose one of these days I'll get around to it. That might even be a better idea than a snake fence. More adventures to follow.

THANK YOU for not only reading this story but these *Author Notes* **as well.**

(I think I've been good with always opening with "thank you." If not, I need to edit the other *Author Notes*!)

RANDOM (*sometimes*) THOUGHTS?

So, apparently, we are speaking about SNAKES this time around.

I (presently) live in Las Vegas, on the Strip, twenty-five stories in the air. If we see a snake, there is a damned problem. I guarantee that.

Now, I didn't always live in Nevada (which I'm sure has snakes. I'm just more worried about the snakes who try to take my money than the ones that bite me on the ankle.) No, I was *born* in the great state of Texas and lived there while I was young…

(Can you see where this is going?)

So, picture this (or don't—it might burn your eyeballs). I'm about eight years old, living in a new subdivision near a set of woods. The woods are being ripped out and bull-dozed, and streets are going in for the next phase of new homes.

But all we have are the cement streets, dirt, and woods about twenty feet from the streets.

This is the time before the internet, video games, and (feels like) damn near electricity. Our best cartoons at the time were *Speed Racer* and *Scooby-doo*.

Spiderman the cartoon (after school) was on, and I wanted to be Spiderman. My friend Jonathan from across the street and I (from somewhere) had appropriated two towels. All it takes (if you have two towels) is to fold them across your skinny shoulders, and you have a cape (okay, a towel-cape).

(Note: You need pretty skinny shoulders and lots of imagination. I had plenty of both.)

Now, it's mid-afternoon. The sun was high in the sky, and we are running around playing superheroes... because that is what you do with a towel at that age... and I see a two-foot-tall pile of dirt near the street. I'm not on the street, so I turn and start running like crazy at the dirt, my little stick legs pumping for all they're worth, and I shove off, attaining a cruising altitude of about three-and-a-half feet. I soar for...probably four feet, my cape swishing in the wind.

Euphoric, I turn around, smiling, to watch Jonathan make the same jump. That's when I see the snake sunbathing on the other side of the dirt pile...the one I couldn't see. I had just jumped *over* the snake.

(Not the same as jumping the shark, but I digress.)

I immediately yell to Jonathan to watch out, *SNAKE!*

Fortunately, he wasn't too sure what I meant, but he soared over the reptile and made it far enough that the snake didn't care.

So, two kids safe, one snake not sure what the hell was going on.

I don't remember what we did next (throw rocks or leave). I would bet we threw rocks…

'Cause what else are you going to do if you are an eight-year-old boy with a cape on?

AROUND THE WORLD IN 80 DAYS

One of the interesting (at least to me) aspects of my life is the ability to work from anywhere and at any time. In the future, I hope to re-read my own *Author Notes* and remember my life as a diary entry.

Cave in the Sky(™) Las Vegas, Nevada, USA

In my office, there are three interior walls and a fourth wall of glass. The glass goes from the floor to the ceiling, allowing me to see outside in all its glory.

The reason I say I'm in a cave in the sky is that I can imagine that the massive wall of glass is the cave opening. I just need to step outside (and fall. Which would suck.)

There would be no cape large enough (I don't think) to save me from *that* stupidity.

I've done ninety-nine stupid things in the past, but that won't be one of them.

FAN PRICING

$0.99 Saturdays (new LMBPN stuff) and $0.99 Wednesday (both LMBPN books and friends of LMBPN books.) Get great stuff from us and others at tantalizing prices.

Go ahead. I bet you can't read just one.

Sign up here: http://lmbpn.com/email/.

HOW TO MARKET FOR BOOKS YOU LOVE
Review them so others have your thoughts, and tell friends and the dogs of your enemies (because who wants to talk to enemies?)... *Enough said ;-)*

Ad Aeternitatem,

Michael Anderle

OTHER SERIES IN THE ORICERAN
UNIVERSE:

SCHOOL OF NECESSARY MAGIC
SCHOOL OF NECESSARY MAGIC: RAINE CAMPBELL
ALISON BROWNSTONE
THE DANIEL CODEX SERIES
THE LEIRA CHRONICLES
I FEAR NO EVIL
FEDERAL AGENTS OF MAGIC
THE UNBELIEVABLE MR. BROWNSTONE
REWRITING JUSTICE
THE KACY CHRONICLES
MIDWEST MAGIC CHRONICLES
SOUL STONE MAGE
THE FAIRHAVEN CHRONICLES

OTHER BOOKS BY JUDITH BERENS

OTHER BOOKS BY MARTHA CARR

JOIN THE ORICERAN UNIVERSE FAN GROUP ON FACEBOOK!